NELLIE'S VICTORY

꙰꙰꙰

Other books by Connie Brummel Crook

Nellie L.
Nellie's Quest
Flight
Meyers' Creek
Laura's Choice
Maple Moon

Nellie's Victory

CONNIE BRUMMEL CROOK

Dear
Aunt Dollie & Art!

Love,
Connie Brummel Crook,
Oct. /99

Stoddart Kids

TORONTO · NEW YORK

Care has been taken to trace ownership of copyright material contained
in this book. The publishers will gladly receive any information that
will enable them to rectify any acknowledgement to copyright holders
in subsequent editions.

Published in Canada in 1999 by
Stoddart Kids,
a division of Stoddart Publishing Co. Ltd.
34 Lesmill Road
Toronto, Canada M3B 2T6
Tel (416) 445-3333 Fax (416) 445-5967
E-mail Customer.Service@ccmailgw.genpub.com

Published in the United States in 2000 by
Stoddart Kids,
a division of Stoddart Publishing Co. Ltd.
180 Varick Street, 9th Floor
New York, New York 10014
Toll free 1-800-805-1083
E-mail gdsinc@genpub.com

Distributed in Canada by
General Distribution Services
325 Humber College Blvd.
Toronto, Canada M9W 7C3
Tel (416) 213-1919 Fax (416) 213-1917
E-mail Customer.Service@ccmailgw.genpub.com

Distributed in the United States by
General Distribution Services
85 River Rock Drive, Suite 202
Buffalo, New York 14207
Toll free 1-800-805-1083
E-mail gdsinc@genpub.com

Canadian Cataloguing in Publication Data
Crook, Connie Brummel
Nellie's victory
ISBN 0-7736-7481-0

1. McClung, Nellie L., 1873–1951 — Juvenile fiction. I Title.

PS8555.R6113N47 1999   jC813'.54   C99-930795-9
PZ7.C8818Ne 1999

*We acknowledge for their financial support of our publishing program the
Government of Canada through the Book Publishing Industry Development
Program (BPIDP), the Canada Council, and the Ontario Arts Council.*

Cover Illustration: David Craig
Cover and Text Design: Tannice Goddard
Layout: Mary Bowness

Printed and bound in Canada

With great thanks to these three,
who helped me to write for publication.

To the late Leslie K. Tarr, who encouraged
me to start,

To Donald G. Bastian, an editor who from the begin-
ning took the time to give reasons for his suggestions,
and

To Kathryn J. Dean, an editor with great patience,
who taught me to correct the problems.

Contents

Acknowledgements

I would like to thank Nellie L. McClung's grand-children, and especially Jane Brown John, the Honourable John McClung, Marcia McClung, and Barrie McClung for their encouragement and for permission to use quotes from Nellie L. McClung's autobiographies, *Clearing in the West* and *The Stream Runs Fast*, as well as her novels and speeches.

A special thanks to University of Toronto Press who gave me permission to make adaptations and reprint quotations from *In Times Like These* and *Purple Springs*, two of Nellie L. McClung's books, for which they have copyright.

Also, thanks to *Maclean's* magazine for permission to quote from them. Thanks to Winnipeg Free Press for permission to quote from *The*

Winnipeg Free Press, The Manitoba Free Press, and *The Winnipeg Tribune.*

Also, a special thanks to Candace Savage for quotes and the use of her research from her wonderful book, *Our Nell, A Scrapbook Biography of Nellie L. McClung.*

I would like to thank very especially Catherine Tarr and her kind friends of Winnipeg who helped her to research for me in Manitoba — and visited sites in Winnipeg, Manitou, and La Riviere. Thank you also for your helpful contacts.

Thanks also go to one of these contacts at Manitou — Diana Vodden, who told me about the Manitou site of Nellie's house and described the history and layout of Manitou, as well as faxing me material from Bob Chalmer's memoirs, from which I obtained the name of Nellie's horse.

Thanks too to Kathryn Dean for editing and encouragement.

PART ONE

Beginnings

1

"Nellie! How can you just sit there *writing*?"

Nellie looked up from her cluttered oak desk and brushed a lock of dark brown hair from her forehead.

"It's the only time I have to write, Mother," she said, turning back to the page in front of her.

"No, Nellie, it's the only time you have to do your morning chores." Mrs. Mooney put her hands on her hips and glared at her daughter. "I always said you'd never make a good wife and mother."

"But," Nellie answered absently, scratching her right temple with the end of her pencil, "I always write a bit in the morning before the children get up." She stared back at her mother then reached for a freshly sharpened pencil. "I love my writing and it does no one any harm."

"That's where you're mistaken! The children are up, and they need you. Jack is trailing around the upstairs hall in his nightshirt, and Florence is screaming to get out of the crib. The only one I didn't hear is the dear baby."

"Oh, Paul's right here," said Nellie, pointing to the two month old tucked into the cradle on the other side of the desk. As she pointed, she brushed the desktop with her arm, smudging her white muslin sleeve with lead and wooden shavings.

"I see the baby there all right," said Mrs. Mooney, budging slightly from her position in the doorway between the study and the dining room. "But he could easily fall out of the cradle at any moment and you wouldn't even notice."

Nellie set her pencil down in exasperation and stared out the window at the swirling snow in the east yard. She wished she'd never asked her mother to help with the children. Mrs. Mooney had been there for only three days and already Nellie could barely stand the nagging.

"Mother," she said, "I have to finish this page. I write in the morning so I can keep a step ahead of the chidren the rest of the day."

"The only way to keep a step ahead of your children is to rise early," Mrs. Mooney answered grimly, smoothing her crisp, white apron over her serviceable navy dress. "When you were a child, I'd be up and going at five. I'd have done a man-size job before *this* time of day." She turned around to glance at the ticking clock in the dining room.

"Why, it's almost eight o'clock! And, my girl, have you forgotten *what* day it is?"

"What day is it?" Nellie asked irritably. She was trying to finish a sentence. "Oh, I remember. Lizzie is coming to take you home today."

"That's not what I meant!" Mrs. Mooney shook her head in dismay. "It's *Monday!*"

"Washday," said Nellie. "Yes, Mother, I do plan to do the wash, but I want to finish this *one* page first."

"I always knew you had a stubborn streak, Nellie, but I thought I'd raised you better than this." Mrs. Mooney turned abruptly and started toward the kitchen. "Well, I'll warm up the porridge for the children. Wes had his at seven before *he* started his day at the drugstore."

Thump! Someone or something had fallen on the floor upstairs.

Nellie and her mother looked straight up to the ceiling. The thump was followed by high-pitched crying. Instantly, Nellie was on her feet, rushing through the dining room into the hallway and up the stairs.

"What did I tell you, Nellie? Something terrible must have happened . . ."

Nellie could no longer hear her mother's scolding voice, for she was taking the stairs two at a time. Halfway across her bedroom, she ran into the crumpled, screaming form of her two-year-old daughter, Florence.

Sweeping the little girl into her arms, Nellie sat down with her on the big bed beside the crib. There was blood all over the child's mouth.

"There, there," Nellie crooned as she tried to see if Florence had knocked out a new tooth. But the bedroom was too dark. She gathered up the child once more and ran downstairs to the kitchen.

Nellie set her little, dark-haired daughter down on the wooden table in the centre of the room. She could get a better look at her there in the light of the coal-oil lamp. Mrs. Mooney had a cold washcloth ready and gently wiped Florence's face. When she pulled the cloth back, the bleeding had stopped.

"She's just cut her lip a little," Mrs. Mooney said calmly. "Look. She's stopped crying already."

"Oh, you poor, poor child," Nellie said softly.

"Now, none of that, Nellie. If you start sympathizing with a child's every little cut and bruise, you'll have them come bawling to you all the time. Take care of their cuts, but don't fuss too much."

Nellie sat down in silence on the rocking chair beside the stove and held the cold cloth over Florence's swelling lower lip. Her mother said no more and started warming up her special oatmeal porridge with the nutmeg flavouring. Then she set a few strips of bacon in a frying pan, and the smell of the porridge and sizzling bacon lifted Nellie's spirits. It was warm there by the stove, and Nellie had to admit there was no porridge quite as good as her mother's.

Outside, the raw west wind, in its race across the open prairie, kept lashing at the white-frame house. That same wind had no doubt passed through Wawanesa to the northwest, rattling the windows on the log home where Nellie had grown up. But now it was crashing against the little place she and Wes had bought on Park Street, at the south end of Manitou. It was mid-January, 1901, the house was on high ground, and had scant protection against the gusts and gales of the Manitoba winter. The closest shelter was the valley of the Pembina River, five miles to the south.

"But Mama always lets me pull the laundry out!"

Nellie's daydreaming was interrupted by the sound of her three year old, Jack, coming down the stairs with Alice, her part-time helper.

"He was into the dirty clothes' hamper in your room, ma'am," said Alice, barely concealing a smile. "He said he was sortin' for the wash."

"I was too," said Jack. "You always let me sort the washing. *Tell* her." He escaped Alice's grasp and ran over to the old plaid couch that stood against the north wall of the kitchen.

"You're right, Jack," said Nellie, "but you have to do the sorting downstairs beside the washing machine, not upstairs! Now wash your hands and get ready for breakfast."

"Yes, Jack, do what your ma'am says." Only five months before, Alice had come to Canada with her parents, who were homesteading on a farm near Manitou. At thirteen, in England, Alice had gone into service as a full-time maid. Now sixteen, she had had very little schooling. So Nellie was giving her grammar lessons in return for part-time housework.

"Come along, Jack," said Mrs. Mooney. "Your porridge is getting cold."

Jack made a face, but dutifully inched toward the breakfast table.

Two hours later, breakfast was over and Jack was happily pulling clothes out of the hamper beside the washing machine. Nellie was stirring whites in a huge copper boiler she and Alice had hoisted onto the stove, and Alice was scrubbing socks on a washboard. Mother, fortunately, was taking care of Florence and Paul in the dining room.

It was a good way to get all three of them out of the way for a bit, thought Nellie as she wiped the perspiration from her forehead and adjusted the bodice of her big-print, red-trimmed apron.

"Do you have any washing soda over there, Alice?" Nellie asked without even turning around. She could not afford to lose a minute.

"No, ma'am," said Alice.

"Well, these stains won't come off completely then, that's all there is to it. I can't spend the entire day doing this!"

Nellie walked over to the washing machine and started pulling out diapers. There were plenty of them now that she had two toddlers and a two-month-old baby. Nellie pushed the diapers through the wringer and went to hang them on one of the clotheslines she had strung across the kitchen. Two shirts and a nightdress were lying on the table. Socks, trousers, and more shirts were hanging over the stove and on the nails by the back door.

"You always were one for the shortcuts," said Mrs. Mooney, waltzing over to where Nellie was slaving away. "And the way you treat that man of yours! Making him bring in water from the well before he leaves for work at seven, and turning your kitchen into chaos with all these ridiculous clotheslines!"

"I agree with you about these lines, Mother," Nellie said, gazing around at them criss-crossing the room. "But what's to be done about it? It's thirty below zero outside. The clothes would only freeze."

"But, Nellie, the frost whitens them."

"That may be, but I'd have a worse mess after I brought them in. They'd thaw out and drip all over the kitchen floor!"

"Well, I used to wait till my family was in bed at night. Then I'd bring the clothes inside to dry *during the night.* In the morning, I'd clear them away before you children were up. Where there's a will, there's a way. You can always tell a clean housekeeper by her wash, Nellie."

"Mother! I do not need to do everything the way you used to!"

Knock! Knock!

Mrs. Mooney and Nellie were interrupted for the second time that morning. Someone was knocking on the *back* door. Strange, Nellie thought. She turned away from her mother, ducked under a couple of lines of drying diapers, twisted around the washing machine, squeezed between two rinse tubs, and opened the door.

As she did so, a great blast of wind came inside, along with her mother-in-law, Mrs. McClung — still as stately as ever. She was wearing a fox-fur hat and a tailored, green woollen coat. There was a yellow-knit scarf around her mouth, which she quickly unwound.

"I'll bet you didn't think you'd see me on a day like this!" She smiled as she turned back and waved at someone outside. A horse and cutter pulled away from the house and headed for Main Street.

"James has a meeting at the Methodist Church across the road, so I decided to stop off to see you." Her husband, James McClung, was now the Methodist minister in the town of Treherne, just northwest of Manitou.

"Well, the place looks as if a cyclone hit it!" Nellie laughed. "But if you can put up with it, you're welcome to sit and have a cup of tea." She pulled back a hanging sheet to reveal her mother. Mrs. Mooney was standing with her hands on her hips, looking slightly ruffled.

"Why, Mrs. Mooney," Mrs. McClung said cheerily, "it's so nice to see you again. I didn't know you were visiting. How are you, my dear?"

"As well as can be expected at my age," said Mrs. Mooney with a sigh. "My arthritis bothers me some, but then what can I expect?"

"I agree it's no fun growing old," said Mrs. McClung, "but then it has its compensations. Just look at the size of this wash! I haven't had one like this since my children were young."

"Did you notice my new washing machine?" Nellie asked proudly, pointing to the metal contraption with its own special wringer, attached to a round tub. Alice was pushing clothes between the rollers with one hand and turning the handle with the other. The freshly washed laundry dropped into the first tub of clear rinse water. The second tub had blueing in it to help whiten the clothes.

"It's wonderful," said Mrs. McClung.

"I bought it with the five dollars I received from the drug company — for an ad I wrote about their headache powders."

"Really!" Mrs. McClung sounded enthusiastic.

"Humph!" said Mrs. Mooney. "She might better have spent her time keeping her house clean."

"Well, I don't agree with you there, Mrs. Mooney. Nellie has a real talent for writing."

"I assure you I have better ideas than writing about headache powders."

"I know you do, and I have something I want you to look at." Mrs. McClung stepped over to her coat and drew a magazine out of one of its pockets. "*Colliers'* has announced a short-story contest for unknown writers," she smiled, waving the magazine in the air. "You really should try for the prize, Nellie. Now, how long do you think it would take you to write a short story?"

"Oh, I can't think about that today." Nellie glanced self-consciously at her mother.

"I'll never understand you, Mrs. McClung," said Mrs. Mooney. "Nellie has quite enough to do without spending her time on such nonsense."

Nellie looked down at the huge pile of dirty clothes still on the floor and over at the steaming copper boiler, and sighed.

"Why not today?" Mrs. McClung went on. "I can take over the washing — with Alice's help."

"But the children?" Nellie said.

"Oh, Alice and I can manage them too. Unless, of course, your mother would like —"

"I'll be leaving shortly," Mrs. Mooney interrupted, looking at the kitchen clock. "Lizzie should have been here before now. My bags are all packed and waiting in the front porch."

"Well, I can manage just fine," said Mrs. McClung. "You forget, Nellie, that I raised three boys and a girl."

Just then there was a knock on the front door and Nellie left the two women staring hard at each other as she went into the hall.

Lizzie flew inside as soon as Nellie opened the door, and gave her sister a big hug. "Hello, Nellie L., I see Mother's bags are here and ready."

"Come in, Lizzie, and bring in the children and Tom."

"I can't. There's a storm coming. I can feel it in the air. We'll have to be on our way. I hope Mother's all ready."

"I am that!" said Mrs. Mooney from over Nellie's shoulder. She took her grey woollen coat from the clothes rack in the hall and stepped into her heavy overshoes. "Well, Nellie," she continued, "I hope you won't listen to Mrs. McClung. But I can't stay around, I have to go." Jack came out, pulling Florence behind him. "Goodbye, Jack and Florence." Then she turned to her daughter. "Try to remember what I've said. Now, goodbye."

Nellie waved as the sleigh pulled away, the bells on the horses' harness jingling. For a brief moment, she felt a twinge of nostalgia for the old farm and the sleigh rides she used to take with her father and her brother, Jack. Then she headed back toward the kitchen where her family duties waited.

Mrs. McClung had already rolled up her sleeves and was putting a new load of clothes into the washing machine. "Now, Nellie," she began, "remember the poor, hard-working women you want to write about? Can they wait to have their story told until your children are grown? I *know* you're capable of writing and raising your family."

"But, Mrs. MClung, I —"

"At this rate, you could be old and grey before you begin to write." Mrs. McClung looked at her with such concern that the usually carefree Nellie began to feel uncomfortable. It was true that she wasn't getting any younger. She'd be twenty-eight in October.

"Life conspires to keep a woman tangled in trifles," Mrs. McClung said, tossing her hair back just a little, "but I'm here to make sure that doesn't happen to you."

"But the children are still so young!"

"How long do you think it would take you to write a short story?" Mrs. McClung insisted.

"A day — I imagine a whole day. In fact, I think I could do a first draft if I had no interruptions for the rest of today. I wrote down a few ideas this morning."

"So you are writing! Well, you must write more. Alice and I can manage fine. Just go to that room of yours. I'll bring your meals."

"I'm afraid it's too cold to write in my regular writing room," Nellie laughed. "My hands get stiff.

For a while, I thought I'd spend the winter thinking, and write like fury in the spring. But now I've taken over that narrow space off the dining room, where it's warmer."

"Good for you. So lend me an apron. You can start work now. This contest is too important to miss."

Finally Nellie nodded and smiled. "You win," she said. She gave Mrs. McClung a crisp, blue-and-yellow apron, offered a few instructions, and retreated.

2

Nellie pulled the golden oak chair up to the matching desk next to the window and picked a sharp pencil out of the cup. The characters she had been writing about that morning began to come back to her as if they were real people.

The central character was twelve-year-old Pearlie Watson, a clever little girl, who took care of her eight brothers and sisters while their mother did washing for well-to-do ladies. Hadn't Nellie always claimed her heroines would belong to the working class, and she would show life from their side of the fence? Yes, she would tell the world how Pearlie and her siblings faced life's hardships with good-humoured joy and fortitude. Pearlie would shoulder her burdens without complaint and be a shining example — not only to the unfortunate, but also to the privileged people around her.

Nellie's hand flew over the pages, and she entered a different world, one of her own making. As she wrote, she almost *became* Pearlie. She no longer saw the storm lashing the windowpanes beside her or heard the wind howling. She didn't even notice the baby crying at feeding time — until Mrs. McClung placed him in her arms. She nursed him with a faraway look in her eyes, still thinking of the *other* children, the deprived Watson children, who lived in an abandoned railway car in a small Manitoba town.

Nellie kept writing as the storm raged. And when Mrs. McClung came for Paul and left a bowl of barley soup on the desk, Nellie barely touched it. She was too busy shivering in the one-room train car with the Watson family, and, as Pearlie, she was trying to come up with a way to get out of the fix they were in.

Suddenly Nellie felt a twitch at the hem of her dress. She looked down and saw part of a white bonnet, and a little hand holding something.

"Florence!" she gasped.

Then she stopped breathing for a moment as she recognized what was in Florence's hand — a pen nib that had fallen from the table. In a moment, Nellie had fled Pearlie's world and snapped back to the reality of her own child's life. Moving her foot carefully so as not to startle her little girl, she grabbed Florence's fist and twisted the pen nib out of her hand. She was just in time.

Florence had been on the point of popping it into her mouth.

"Waaaahhh!" Florence began to wail. She was not one to give up easily. Nellie was cradling her in her left arm and scribbling with her right hand when Mrs. McClung came to the rescue.

The sky was darkening outside, and Nellie had not yet reached the high point of her story. She was in danger of not being finished before Wes came home — and who knew when she would have another chance to complete the tale? She wrote like lightning and was just coming to the climax when she felt someone tugging at her sleeve.

"Mother?" It was Jack, with a look of great urgency on his face. "Mother, do geese hibernate in the winter? I was just wondering because I can't see any outside."

"Oh, no, Jack," Nellie stifled her laughter, "they fly south."

"*I'm* going to learn how to fly when I grow up."

"Good idea!" Nellie said absently as she continued to scribble in the near-darkness. Jack seemed happy with the answer and ran back to the kitchen.

Nellie raised her head. Outside the window, it was pitch-dark, but a coal-oil lamp cast light on the last few lines of her story. Mrs. McClung must have brought the lamp in. Nellie leaned back, exhausted, as the smell of fresh-roasted chicken and the sound of Wes's voice came from the kitchen.

"Would you believe it, Mother?" Wes was saying

in a weary voice. "I had to give anaesthesia today. Yes, Dr. MacCharles asked me to help. He operated for appendicitis — right on the kitchen table. He couldn't find anyone else to administer the anaesthetic. So guess who . . ."

Nellie jumped from her chair and rushed through the doorway. "Wes!" she shouted as she raced through the dining room to the kitchen. "How did you do it? Who was the patient?"

Wes turned to his wife. He looked tired and his face was whiter than usual. But he was still the tall, slim, athletic man she'd married. He ran his fingers back through his red hair and looked at Nellie with his steady, blue eyes.

"Don't worry, Nellie. He's fine now. But it was your brother, Jack."

"I didn't even know he was sick!"

"He wasn't. It hit very suddenly. The other doctors were out on call, so Dr. MacCharles sent a boy to get me. I rode to the farm, and the doctor operated right there on the kitchen table. He had to, or the appendix would have burst. And then we could have done nothing but watch Jack die of the poison."

"How's Barbara?" Nellie asked. Jack and Barbara had been married five years ago, soon after Nellie and Wes. They now had a son, Harry, and two daughters, Mary and Ruth. "I must go help."

"No need for that. I went up to Treesbank on my way back and told Barbara's family. Two of her sisters set off for the farm right away. And Bob Ingram is taking care of the chores."

Nellie sank into the big rocking chair by the stove. "Is Jack going to be all right?"

"Yes, he came along fine. And out of the anaesthetic, too, I might add. But I must say, I didn't enjoy giving it. The worst is that the doctors will probably be after me to help them from now on. I wasn't trained for this, and I don't like doing it."

"We do have three doctors in this town. You'd think they could handle it," Nellie sighed.

"Let's hope so." Wes's mouth was drawn in a tight line and his eyes looked strained.

Mrs. McClung took a steaming pan of scalloped potatoes from the oven and set it on the table. "Let's eat," she said. "A good meal will help." She turned back to a side table, picked up a platter of carved chicken — white and dark meat — and set it down beside a pitcher of gravy, a bowl of spicy dressing, and a dish of homemade cranberry sauce. The red-checked oilcloth shone cheerfully in the light of a coal-oil lamp.

How wonderful to have a meal all ready for you, Nellie thought, sinking into her chair at the end of the table.

"Wes, why don't you take the day off tomorrow and go curling?" Nellie said after he'd given thanks. "You need a change."

"I can't, Nellie. I have to double-check all my assistant's prescriptions. I just can't get away from the store for long. Now, tell me, Nellie, what have you been doing all day?"

"Why? Do you think I was doing something unusual?"

"Well, I know you were doing *something*. I can tell by the look on your face!"

"I've written a short story," Nellie beamed. "Do you want to hear part of it?"

"Yes, Nell, you always tell a great tale — but wait till after supper. You have competition now!"

"All I have left to do is copy it out neatly in ink tomorrow and send it away."

"I'll come again and see that you do," said Mrs. McClung in a soft but determined voice. She looked at Nellie with pride.

The children were all in bed, and Mrs. McClung had gone home with her husband. Nellie and Wes were sitting on the old couch against the north wall.

"We really should replace this couch," he said, looking at the end of a spring sticking up through the plaid upholstery right next to him.

"There's nothing wrong with it," frowned Nellie. "Why should we get a new one?"

"Just take a look at this spring!"

"Oh, I know, but I like this old couch. Whenever I have visitors, they can just come and sit over here with a cup of tea — and I can keep working at the stove."

"But look at the thing, Nell! It's a wreck!"

"It can be fixed."

"Well, if you're that attached to it . . . . But why don't we discuss that later? You need to read me your story now."

"I don't know, Wes. Maybe it's better if I revise it again first. I wrote it in such a hurry."

"Oh, go on, Nell, read to me." Wes slouched back on the couch.

"How can I refuse?" Nellie reached over to the table and picked up the pages. "But I think I should explain first. The story's about a poor family with nine children. Their father is a handyman and a hard worker, but he was very seriously injured the previous autumn. He's only now recovering. Mrs. Watson, their mother, works as a maid to help support the family, while Pearlie, the oldest daughter, keeps house six days a week and takes care of the children. The youngest is Danny. He's four. They barely have enough to eat, and snowstorms have nearly covered their so-called home, a former CPR boxcar."

"A CPR boxcar!" Wes guffawed. "You do have a wild imagination."

"No, Wes," Nellie said reprovingly. "You know people lived in that car over on the siding at the Manitou train station for a few months last fall."

"But that was fall. No one could survive a Manitoba winter in a boxcar!"

"Well, it's just a story, and besides, I'm sure I've heard of . . ."

"Go on, Nell, tell me the rest."

"Well, to pass the cold, dreary, winter hours when the children are trying to keep warm inside their little home, Pearlie makes up a story about a wonderful, rich woman, known as the 'pink lady,' who will fulfill all their dreams. And, of course, each child has a dream of his own."

"Hmm. I think I see where this is going," Wes said. "You always were a dreamer of dreams!"

"It isn't *all* dreams. One of the brothers, Jimmy, delivers milk to a wealthy woman in the town, and she takes an interest in helping the youngest boy, Danny. I'll read you the part where she asks to see him. Just listen . . .

"'Will you bring Daniel to see me tomorrow, James?' she said . . . . 'I would like to speak to his young mind and endeavour to plant the seeds of virtue and honesty in that fertile soil.'

"When Jimmy got home he told Pearlie of his interview with the pink lady, as much as he could remember. The only thing that he was sure of was that she wanted to see Danny, and that she had said something about planting seeds in him.

"Jimmy and Pearlie thought it best not to mention Danny's proposed visit to their mother, for they knew that she would be fretting about his clothes, and would be sitting up mending and sewing for him when she should be sleeping. So they resolved to say 'nothin' to nobody.'

"The next day their mother went away early to wash for the Methodist minister's wife, and that was always a long day's work. Then the work of preparation began on Danny."

Nellie looked up at Wes, who'd stretched his long legs out toward the stove to keep his feet warm. He was smiling. "This story is unmistakably you! Children, washday . . ."

"Don't tease me, Wes."

"I'm not finished. It *is* about that — the everyday things — but it's also about a woman who cares for people and does something to help. And guess who *that's* like! You don't just make life wonderful for your family. You help people outside these four walls, too."

"You're flattering me, Wes, but I can match you! You could show most men a thing or two about how to treat their wives. They don't respect the women they married the way you respect me. You're an exception, Mr. McClung."

"Thanks, Nell. Now, back to the story."

"Well, Pearlie continues gleefully to dress poor Danny for his visit to the rich woman. She melts snow for bath water, then washes Danny and dresses him in the best borrowed article of clothing from each child until he is shining, clean and ready.

"The mischievous Danny, of course, wins the heart of the rich lady and demands that his sister, Pearlie, tell this woman the tale of the pink lady, who leaves gifts for the whole family. The rich woman is, indeed, touched by the story and resolves to help this poor family by becoming their 'pink lady.' She sees that sowing seeds of thought in Danny is far too idealistic and that his greatest need right now is not for ideas but for help against cold and hunger."

"And what's the story called?" Wes asked with a twinkle in his eye.

"Sowing Seeds in Danny."

"I see why you want to call it that, but I don't know if it makes sense as a title."

"Well, maybe I'll change my mind, but not right now. Anyway, here I am talking on and on — and after you having such a hard day. Let's get some sleep." Nellie picked up the coal-oil lamp from the table and headed toward the hall.

Wes nodded and followed her. As they walked up the stairs, the wind battered the windowpanes and howled its way across the open prairie.

3

Nellie went to the gilt-edged hall mirror at the front door and put on her white leghorn hat with the red velvet flowers. She brushed a bit of dust off her new navy-blue-and-white-striped voile dress trimmed with Valenciennes lace. It was perfect for a July meeting, and it made Nellie feel like a different woman — not the harried housewife Mrs. McClung had found at home last January!

Nellie was determined to be as easy as possible on the eye, for today she was to be the speaker at an important meeting of the Woman's Christian Temperance Union, a group of women helping women. The meeting was to be held in the Manitou Town Hall.

"Mama, Mama, come quick!" It was Jack. His blond curls shone in the slanted light of midmorning.

"I'm in a terrible rush, Jack, so tell me, what is it?"

"I *found* it!"

"Found *what?*"

"A lake! In the pantry!"

Nellie paled and turned abruptly away from the door. She knew Jack had not found a lake; he'd found the cistern. And one of the children could easily fall in if it was open.

"Look, Mama, it's right here!"

Nellie breathed a long sigh of relief as she saw that the lid to the cistern was only slightly ajar. And with typical foresight, her oldest son had tied little Paul to the door to keep him safe. The seven month old could now crawl almost as quickly as his two older siblings walked.

"What a discovery, Jack," Nellie said, "but it is very dangerous to move that lid, so don't touch it again!" She hadn't thought Jack was strong enough to budge the cover — even a little. Wes would have to add a weight to it.

"But, Ma . . ."

Nellie untied the baby quickly and handed him to Alice, who had just come in to help for the day. Paul immediately grasped a lock of Alice's light brown hair in his tiny fists.

Nellie adjusted the lid and set a heavy crock of butter on it. "We're going to take our food to the Town Hall for a meeting today," she said. "And we're going in the buggy because I have to drive to the train station right afterwards."

"Can I come? Can I?"

"Yes, Jack. You're all coming to see where your

mama is speaking this afternoon. But after that, you're staying at home with Alice. Now move! Quick as lightning!"

Nellie sounded impatient, even to herself. At moments like this, she wondered whether she really *could* write, work for women, and care for her family. But there was no point in worrying about that now . . . she had too much to do.

Nellie went over to the kitchen table and picked up a blue-willow serving dish. It was filled to the brim with creamy, golden scalloped potatoes. Dishes and plates full of sliced meats and steaming vegetables were already stashed in the buggy, waiting to be delivered.

Out on Main Street, the July morning was bright and the scent of wild roses mixed with the freshness of the prairie earth. A few inches of rain had just fallen. There was nothing more delightful to a prairie dweller than this. Nellie revelled in it and gave Jasper's back a slap with the reins. Jasper was a good-tempered horse who limped a bit.

Alice and the three children were snuggled up together next to Nellie, singing their songs. It warmed Nellie's heart to hear them. She sighed, realizing once again how fortunate she was. She and Wes were always on speaking terms. The rent was paid. Although Manitou was small, life was never dull in the little town. True, she had her clothesline breaks and jellies that would not jell — and she'd seen men die from drinking, and animals suffer from starvation. But her life was very happy, all in all. Why should she not think well of the world?

As she approached the Town Hall, however, she saw something that made her furious. Two banners had been slung across the front entrance. On them, someone had scrawled in black soot: WCTU — Women Continually Torment Us, and Women, Go Home! No need for you in Manitou!

Nellie flung the reins to Alice, jumped down from the buggy, and ripped the banners down. The soot lifted off them and floated away into the clear morning air.

"It's good you saw them banners first, ma'am," said Alice.

Jack jumped out of the buggy and stood beside his mother, trying to read the sooty lettering.

Nellie started to fold the banners, with the remnants of the black soot facing in. Then she turned to Jack. "Watch your little sister," she said. "Look! She's already trying to get over the side of the buggy!"

"No!" Florence pouted as Alice grabbed the hem of her green gingham dress. Florence, at two, was already showing some of her mother's strong will.

Nellie pushed the offending banners under the seat and took her dish of scalloped potatoes into the hall.

The noon train would be bringing seventy-five delegates to the WCTU Convention from all parts of Manitoba, and the Manitou WCTU had asked Nellie to give the opening speech. She was excited and afraid all at the same time. She'd spoken to local groups before, but never to such a crowd.

Several delegates were coming from Winnipeg, ninety miles away.

As she hurried back to her buggy, the red velvet flowers on her leghorn hat bending in the breeze, she nearly ran into Mrs. Wheeler, who lived across from the McClungs on Park Street. She was a tall, thin woman with a lined face, but she no longer showed the strains of living with her husband's drunkenness.

"Well, how's our Nell?" she smiled warmly. "I'm so looking forward to hearing you speak this afternoon."

"Thank you, Mrs. Wheeler, I'll try my best." Nellie smiled, trying to hide her nervousness.

Mr. Wheeler had once been a farmer, but he'd also been such a big drinker that he'd lost the family farm. About five years ago, he'd had a dramatic conversion to Christ at a revival meeting. Since that night, he'd never touched a drop. Now he was part owner of the Manitou lumber mill and was also one of the most steadfast deacons in the Methodist Church. Nellie smiled and waved to him sitting in his buggy. She suddenly felt a lot less nervous. As long as she could do *something* to help men like Wheeler, nothing else mattered.

"I'll be cheering for you today, Nell!" Nellie turned and saw Mrs. Brown, a widow from Wawanesa, who had now bought a farm near Manitou. She was president of the local WCTU. "Are you nervous?"

"I was a bit, earlier today, but I just saw Mrs. Wheeler, and that inspired me to labour on!"

"Yes, her husband is such a success story.

Besides, Nellie, you'll be brilliant, as usual!" Mrs. Brown headed toward the street, the July sun softening the lines on her tanned face. She had run a farm alone since her husband's death, but she almost always appeared calm and neatly dressed. Her slightly greying hair was tied in a French knot at the nape of her neck.

Nellie slapped the reins on Jasper's back. She had only a few short minutes to drop Alice and the children at the house a block away and then head straight for the CPR station at the north end of town.

As the noon train roared into Manitou station, belching steam and coal dust, Nellie looked proudly at the members of the local WCTU who were waiting to greet the out-of-town delegates. These women did not confine themselves to diapers and prams. They were responsible wives and mothers who felt that women and men should work together in the home and in public life.

The seventy-five delegates stepped down from the train — a great assembly of love and energy ready to take on anything that threatened their children and their communities. They were the White Ribboners, women who had taken the pledge to abstain from all forms of alcohol. They were aware of the effects of drunkenness on families and did everything they could to help people who suffered because of drinking.

Nellie noticed that most of them were also slim and fit from the hard manual work that was a regular part of their lives. Nellie, only five feet tall and not as wiry, looked at them with admiration and some fear. Would farmers' wives want to hear from someone who had left the farm and now enjoyed an easier life? And would the more sophisticated women from Winnipeg want to listen to a girl from the country?

The delegates moved toward the waiting buggies, a sea of womanly strength. Many were dressed in henrietta cloth skirts and crisp white blouses fastened with brooches. All wore the white ribbon of temperance.

"It fairly takes your breath away, doesn't it, Nell?" said Mrs. Brown, who'd come up beside her quietly.

"Yes, but it's life and breath to see them, too. Someday great changes will be brought about as a result of these small beginnings."

As the buggies whisked the women away to the Town Hall, the sun beat down as if in blessing, and meadowlarks sang in the greening fields.

"I wanted to leave him then, but I couldn't, for fear he'd forget to feed the hens."

Nellie turned away from the table heaped with shiny platters and bowls full of food fit for queens — and recognized the wife of a farmer she knew. Even during harvest time, that woman's husband was sometimes drunk for days on end. She was speaking to Mrs. Wheeler, the perfect person to console and advise her. The farmer's wife reminded Nellie of Mrs. Sayers. Her daughter,

Sarah, had been one of Nellie's brightest and most pleasant pupils, but her father had been a drunkard who'd finally died from his habit. He'd frozen to death in his sleigh in a blizzard.

The room was abuzz with women engaged in serious discussions, heart-to-heart chats, and hilarious laughter. The meeting was getting off to a good start. Food always helped, thought Nellie. Tables had been set up in a U around the main room of the Town Hall.

Heavy blue-trimmed china platters held chicken, sliced and jellied, fresh from the cold cellars of Manitou. Sugar-coated hams lay on beds of fresh garden lettuce. And there were bowls and bowls of potatoes. Some were scalloped, some were made into potato salad, and some were whipped soft and fluffy with real cream skimmed off fresh milk.

On a smaller table next to the podium, the pies were displayed in all their glory: lemon heaped with white meringue, raspberry, saskatoon-berry, and even a few made with dried apples shipped from Ontario. One thing was certain: the women of the Manitou WCTU had prepared a feast that could not fail to uplift their guests.

Who said women couldn't organize?

As Nellie was contemplating the great things the WCTU could do, she almost bumped into little Jennie Gills, one of the local members.

"Excuse me, Jennie," said Nellie.

"It's not your fault!" Jennie responded. "It's hard to avoid me these days. I'll be having my baby any time now."

"Well, if things start happening during the meeting, we'll get you home in no time!"

"It won't happen that fast, Nellie!"

Nellie wondered how Jennie could appear so calm and cheerful. After her last baby had been delivered, her husband had gotten roaring drunk, and threatened to kill her and the child. Only through sheer force had Dr. MacCharles and the midwife been able to subdue him. Mr. Gills had been remorseful for months afterwards, but who knew what lay ahead for Jennie and the second baby?

Nellie headed over to take a look at the dessert table, smiling as she went. She'd just remembered something. If Jennie's husband pulled any more tricks, he'd have to face down the three WCTU women billeted at his home, the seventy-two other delegates, and all the members of the local WCTU. Perhaps things would go better for Jennie this time.

Nellie's thoughts were interrupted again as another WCTU member brushed passed her.

"Pardon me," she said. "I was so enchanted by those desserts, I nearly ploughed you under!" In spite of the woman's rough language, she looked cheerful and businesslike in a crisp navy-blue dress. "Please excuse me, Mrs. . . . ."

"Mrs. McClung . . . Nellie."

"And I'm Mrs. White, from Carman."

"Carman! I've heard they're building a new hotel there."

"Yes . . . and that spells trouble! It's just one more watering hole where men can spend their families' money after they've sold the wheat crop."

"Is there any opposition?"

"From me there is! I own and operate the general store in Carman. Every penny's worth of liquor that goes down those farmers' gullets means a penny of sales lost for me. Besides, my sister's husband came home one night three months ago dead drunk, and he beat her to within an inch of her life. I'll stand for no more shenanigans that lead to tragedies like that."

Mrs. White smiled grimly at Nellie and then continued on to the dessert table.

At that very moment, Nellie looked up into the smiling eyes of a pretty but serious-looking woman. She was dressed in bright red silk, with a wide white-lace collar. The white ribbon pinned to her dress appeared even larger and more prominent than the others in the room. A beautiful gold watch hung from a long golden chain about her neck.

"It's wonderful that you could come to Manitou," said Nellie, stepping forward and extending her hand. "I'm Nellie McClung."

"Nellie McClung! I think I know your name."

Nellie tried not to stare in surprise.

"Yes . . . did you write a column a couple of years ago in *The Manitou Mercury* about the conditions of farm wives?"

"Why, yes, I wrote one or two."

"I remember — *The lives of country people are filled with disappointments, long hours, and grey monotony . . .*"

"What an excellent memory! That was the lead for one of my articles."

"Well, I'm Mrs. Claudia Nash, from Winnipeg,"

said the woman in red, as she moved over to the
main-course table and filled her plate with two
slices of jellied chicken, a pile of cucumber pickles
and all three kinds of potatoes. "You know, when I
read about the farm wives, I couldn't help thinking of the poor factory girls in Winnipeg. What I
wouldn't give to share this meal with them."

"Factory workers?" Nellie asked, raising her eyebrows.

"Yes. They're even worse off than farm women,
I believe," Mrs. Nash said. "They work hard too —
but in far less healthy conditions. The very air they
breathe is filled with germs. Consumption is ram-
pant in the factories."

Nellie was staring at her, open-mouthed. She
hadn't heard of this problem before.

Mrs. Nash continued, "There's often only one
toilet for fifty workers, and it's for men *and*
women, I might add. Anyway, the workers are not
allowed to use the toilet during their working
shift, which lasts a whole morning or afternoon.
And sometimes the lineups are too long for everyone to get to them during their half-hour lunch."

Nellie gaped at the woman in shocked silence.

"Oh, my dear, am I spoiling your meal? I didn't
mean to. I just get carried away sometimes. Young
girls go into these places in the bloom of health
and emerge ten months later, filled with consumption and headed for an early grave."

"But can't anything be done about it? Aren't
there factory inspectors?"

"There are — *men* in charge. And I've
complained, but nothing has been done. I've even

written to our premier, Sir Rodmond Roblin — a pompous, sheltered man."

"Did he not answer your letter?"

"Oh, he answered all right, but the thing was useless. Filled with literary allusions and empty promises. He did nothing about it, of course — but I'm sorry. This isn't the time or place to talk about it."

"Oh, but it *is*, Mrs. Nash. It is *exactly* the place to talk about it! And I hope to hear more. I have to go now to prepare for my welcoming speech, but I do want to talk with you later."

"I'll look forward to that," said Mrs. Nash. "In fact, Nellie, I wonder if we could keep in touch. May I write to you? I see you'd appreciate hearing about the struggle. And we could encourage each other."

"Yes, do," said Nellie. "I would like that."

Mrs. Nash turned then to speak to a woman who had come up beside her.

Nellie went to the kitchen to set down her half-empty plate, and was heading for the small office to freshen up when a younger member called out to her.

"Mrs. McClung," she said. "It's me . . . Sarah Sayers."

Nellie had not even recognized her. She was not at all like the thin wisp of a child she'd taught five years before in Wawanesa. Sarah still had the same beautiful, big blue eyes, but her whitish blonde hair had grown thick and golden, hanging in two braids down her back. Nellie realized she must be seventeen now.

"Sarah, it's wonderful to see you. I had no idea you were a member of the WCTU."

"Yes, I'm a member up in Roland. My mother and I have a farm there."

Nellie remembered now. After Sarah's father had died, she and her mother had moved away from the community and their tragic memories.

"It's good to know we have young recruits like you, Sarah," Nellie said. "Let's chat after the meeting."

"Yes, and come visit us in Roland sometime! It's not that far away."

Sarah went to talk to another delegate, and Nellie continued into the office to get ready. She looked at her dress in the wall mirror. Yes, the navy and white stripes gave her a crisp, efficient look. And that was softened nicely by the Valenciennes lace. It gave her confidence to know that she at least looked competent.

But then Nellie remembered the first time she'd spoken to a ladies' group, and she began to feel very nervous. She'd been so overconfident then she'd forgotten all her main points!

Back out in the dining room, Nellie watched the women walking in twos and threes to the seats in front of the podium. She saw the high resolve in their faces and felt another wave of fear. Had she really been called to give her message to women all over Manitoba? Now that she'd met Mrs. Nash, she was worried that she did not have a broad enough understanding of women's lives outside her own community.

But it was too late to back out now. She walked

over to the podium. Mrs. Brown had come forward and asked the audience to rise. They did so quickly and repeated the membership pledge: "I hereby solemnly promise, God helping me to abstain from all . . . liquors . . . and to employ all means to discourage the use and traffic in the same." Then the women sat down again while Mrs. Brown briefly introduced Mrs. Nellie L. McClung as the afternoon speaker.

Nellie rose and walked slowly to the front. Then she lifted her head and faced the large group of serious-looking women. She saw tired, lined faces, but eyes full of hope. Nellie felt a great surge of love for these people, so burdened with concern for others.

"Some claim," Nellie began, "that a woman's place is in the home, that she should not become involved in affairs of state."

Mrs. Nash leaned forward in her front-row chair and listened intently.

"Some claim," Nellie continued, "that a woman should 'mind her own business.' But what is minding one's own business? It's only a second-rate virtue. It's just an excuse for laziness, coldness, and neglect!"

A few older women sitting at the back coughed and looked down at the floor. Nellie sensed a bit of disapproval, but that was not going to stop her.

"It is not so much a woman's duty to bring children into the world as it is to change the world she is bringing them into."

The audience stirred, and all the women except the disapproving ones at the back burst into a round of spontaneous applause.

Nellie waited for the clapping to die down, then went on. "The very best work that any woman can do in the world is to bring up her children in the nurture and admonition of the Lord. But that is no excuse for 'minding one's own business.' The woman who wants to bring her children up to manhood and womanhood in purity and goodness, and wants to see them have a good chance in life — is the woman who wants to see other people's children get their chance too."

One of the disapproving women at the back looked up again, and this time, she seemed to be listening carefully.

"It is never acceptable to simply 'mind one's own business' — but in this day, it is a crime to do so. By minding their own business, women who live in happy homes are condemning other women to misery and sometimes early death. By doing nothing to stop men from drinking, women who 'mind their own business' stand by and watch as women and children are swallowed by fear, dire poverty, and suffering. And why are these women and children suffering? Because their men have been bewitched into a love affair with whiskey!"

Jennie Gills squirmed in her chair, but then looked up at Nellie with a bit of hope in her eyes.

"I know why people drink. It answers something in their blood, some craving for excitement and change. We are a farming community, and life on our farms can be hard and monotonous. That's why men try to escape by getting drunk." Nellie looked over at Mrs. Brown. There was a woman who knew how hard farm life could be — but she did not race out to the hotel for a drink whenever she felt she had too much work to do.

"These men escape for a little while. But what happens to their women and children? At best, they live in poverty. At worst, they are beaten or killed. When they drink, loving fathers, brothers, and sons turn into negligent and violent monsters."

Mrs. Nash straightened up in her chair and nodded. A hand shot up from the middle of the audience. It belonged to Mrs. Ingram. Nellie cringed inwardly. She had no idea why her mother's critical friend came to these meetings. Mrs. Ingram saw the WCTU as little more than a pack of troublemakers. And now she was no doubt going to spoil Nellie's first speech to WCTU women from all over Manitoba!

Mrs. Ingram plunged right in. Her white hair, once blonde, was pulled back in a braided bun that made her look even more determined than she already was. "But, Nellie, we can't stop them," she said. "If they want to drink, there's not a thing we can do except hope they'll change their ways."

Nellie smiled. She had been planning to say something about exactly that. She could not have asked for a better setup.

"You're absolutely right, Mrs. Ingram. We cannot stop this foolish destruction by wagging our fingers and clicking our tongues. Prohibition is a hard-sounding word. So it is worthless as a rallying cry, hard as a locked door or going to bed without your supper. If we are to convince men to stop drinking, we must offer them something more."

Applause broke out again and Nellie's heart filled with joy. With a response like this, she really *could* inspire women to change the world.

"Look at the Salvation Army. They know the compelling power of rhythm and light and warmth and friendliness. They know the drawing power of coffee and sandwiches and the beat of a drum. They know how to fight the powers of evil, and we, the Temperance women, need to do the same. We must fight fire with fire.

"When we make our voices heard, we will stop the liquor traffic. And the money saved can make life much more attractive for both men and women. We can have recreation grounds, games, orchestras, folk dances, better houses, better farms, new hopes for a new world. Britain's former prime minister, the late William Gladstone, once said that he could pay the country's great national debt if he only had a sober England. Just think what we Canadians, who have no great national debt, could do for a sober Canada!

"But we will do nothing by minding our own business.

"I believe God did intend us to be happy and comfortable, clothed, fed, and housed, and there is no sin in comfort, unless we let it make us unfeeling, idle, and selfish. Then it can destroy us.

"And in this vein, I would like to close with a prayer. From plague, pestilence, and famine," Nellie prayed, "from battle, murder, sudden death, and all forms of cow-like contentment, Good Lord, deliver us!"

As Nellie sat down, she hardly heard the long applause. She was still seeing the faces of the women, and suddenly she realized for the first time that she had the power of speech to move others.

She knew, too, with a certainty that she was committed to a long fight and a hard one.

4

Sept. 16, 1901

Dear Mrs. McClung:

  We thank you for entering our contest but regret to inform you that although your story passed all our preliminary readers and was held until the last, it did not win the prize. You have written a delightful story with humour and originality, but it is rather too juvenile for our purposes.

Yours truly,
Henry McCormick

Nellie's heart sank. A whole day of writing and neglecting her children — and nothing to show for it! And to make things worse, it had taken the judges a long time to inform her of their decision.

A brisk September breeze picked the letter up

and blew it onto the floor. Nellie snatched it up again. A rejection letter was the last thing she needed today. Her mother and Lizzie were due to arrive for a visit later that afternoon. But at least that left no time to mope! Nellie stuffed the letter under the manuscript, which she'd already set next to a mixing bowl full of flour on the kitchen table.

Fortunately, Alice was away helping her parents on the farm, so Nellie did not have to explain her disappointment to anyone.

She decided to go to the cellar to get some eggs. But just as she was turning away, she noticed another letter beside the manuscript. Nellie had no idea who it could be from. It was on ivory, personalized stationery. "Mrs. Claudia . . . *Nash!*" Mrs. Nash had sent a short thank-you note after the WCTU meeting in July, but had not written since.

Nellie took a knife out of the drawer in the cupboard and opened the envelope.

Dear Nellie, fellow temperance fighter:
First of all, where did you learn to speak like that? The way you spoke when we all came down to Manitou for the WCTU meeting — you brought the house down!

Nellie smiled. After that rejection letter, it was good to hear a compliment.

I'd like you to bring down another house, too, Nellie. Can't you come to Winnipeg right away? My good friend Lillian Thomas goes to the Manitoba legislature —

that's the House I mean — as part of her job. She's a reporter for The Winnipeg Free Press. *And that place needs a lot of housecleaning!*

Here's the latest. There's a young Conservative, name of Jonas Babcock. He's out to impress Roblin. No doubt has his eye on a Cabinet post. As Lillian was rushing out of the building to file yesterday's story, she overheard him offering this marvelous view of women to another MPP: "Women were made to charm us, to inspire us — cheer us, but certainly not to rival us!" With thinking like that, it's no wonder we're in such a mess.

Nellie carried the letter to the cellar, picked up two eggs, and started back upstairs, reading.

And then there's the premier. He was quoted in the Telegram *the other day, extolling the virtues of women like his mother, who realized their weaker state and stayed at home, where they could actually do some good. I wish he'd stay home! He'd do a lot more good there. For one thing, he's done a lot of damage to our cause. When that rotter took on the leadership of the Conservative Party two years ago, public opinion clearly supported prohibition. But the old charmer delayed legislation against the liquor interests by calling for another public vote on the matter.*

And speaking of delays, do you think that man will give me an appointment? I desperately need to talk to him about the North End slums. You go up there and see excrement oozing out of the outhouses. There are no sewers. And families sleep three and four to a bed in ramshackle houses. I have connections through Lillian

*Thomas and her sister Frances Beynon, but the last time
I was scheduled to see the premier, his secretary phoned to
say he had a speaking engagement at some confounded
land developers' luncheon. Typical. The man made so
much money in the grain trade, he thinks of no one but
his fellow businessmen. He's deaf to our appeals.*

*And the women's movement? It was stronger in the
1890s. Since then, it's just been going downhill.*

*We need your help, Nellie! When are you coming to
Winnipeg?*

Nellie sighed and tucked the letter into the
pocket of her apron. I think I need *her* help more!
she thought, looking at the pots and pans piled up
in the kitchen sink.

"Here's a whole bunch of feathers for
Florence!" said Jack. He was in the sitting room,
but his voice carried all the way into the kitchen.
"And some for me!" he went on. "And some for
Mama! And, let's see, who else needs feathers?"

Nellie jumped up and rushed through the dining room into the sitting room. And there stood
Jack in majestic glory, surveying the scene, surrounded by piles and piles of feathers. They were
goose feathers, Nellie noticed, so they must have
come from her pillows.

"What are you doing, Jack? What a mess!"

Jack looked at her innocently, almost as if asking
for approval. "I'm getting enough feathers to make
wings, so I can fly," he said, by way of explanation.

"What?" Nellie did not know whether to scold
him or to laugh. So she just stared in amazement.
"Jack, once and for all, you cannot learn to fly. So

just give up this idea. These feathers all have to go back into the pillows — and now!"

Jack paused and considered this as his mother stared steadily at him. "Oh, all right — but I'm not you're boy anymore! You don't love me!"

"Of course I do. But all the same, you have to put every feather back into these pillows."

Nellie headed back out to the kitchen. She'd check on Jack again in a few minutes. She had no time to discuss things with him now. Mother, the most spotless housekeeper in the world, and Lizzie, the next most spotless housekeeper in the world, were already on their way — and Mother would have lots to say if she noticed the least speck of dust anywhere. Let alone a sea of feathers!

Nellie grabbed a washcloth. Then she started to scrub the kitchen table with a vengeance. It was just one o'clock, but she had to hurry. Mother now lived with Lizzie and her family, and this past year, they had moved to a farm east of Holland, which was thirty-five miles northwest of Manitou. They would all be staying the night, for it was almost a day's trip by horse and buggy to their home.

Nellie had just put Florence and Paul down for their afternoon naps — and Jack was about to go next door to play with a friend. Paul always slept like an angel, but Florence was a feisty, curious girl. Today, she was especially restless and had refused to put her head on her pillow until Nellie gave her a picture book. It was a little story that Nellie had made up about her life back on the farm. She'd drawn pictures of herself as a child with Nap, the dog, running over the fields.

Nellie glanced briefly out of the window, and saw Abe Smith, a well-known drunk, stumbling along the street. He did not often drink to excess, but when he did, he became helpless. Nellie usually took him in until he sobered up, because he was a bachelor without relatives nearby to help him. But today, he'd just have to spend the afternoon sleeping on a bench in Coronation Park.

Nellie stepped over to the iron stove and with her long poker shuffled the wood around so it would break into a hot blaze. Hurrying across the kitchen, she seasoned the beef roast she'd bought that very morning from the meat shop down the street. She pushed it into a roasting pan and slid the pan into the oven.

Nellie washed her hands in the wash pan and dried them on the roller towel. At last, she felt more content. After all, the WCTU meeting had been a success, and no matter what publishers decided, she still had a vision of a new world. She knew her calling.

Just the same, she couldn't bear to tell anyone about her manuscript — not yet. She grabbed the pages and stashed them under a piece of blue gingham broadcloth on top of the sewing machine that sat just inside the dining-room door. She did her sewing in there, for the materials often fell to the floor as she worked and that floor was always cleaner than the one in the kitchen.

Nellie could not help laughing when she thought how different her life was from her mother's. Letitia Mooney was a dour, practical Scot, who believed that women were meant to serve the menfolk of the family. She would never be convinced differently by her daughter, by a Mrs. Nash or, for that matter, by a woman as prominent as the British suffragette Emmeline Pankhurst. Nellie chuckled at the thought of her mother having a talk with Emmeline about the role of women. She would no doubt listen for about a minute, and then scold her.

Nellie was just putting the broom back in the pantry closet when she heard a loud knock on the back door. She could not believe her relatives had arrived so soon. They must have left home at sunup.

She hurried over and pulled the door open. Three beaming faces smiled up at her. One belonged to Lizzie's George, who was six months older than Jack; the other two belonged to his sisters, Olive and Clara, aged two and three.

"Mommy and Grandma are coming!" George announced.

Nellie looked over to the back shed to see Lizzie, still as slender as a willow, helping her mother down from the buggy.

"Where's Jack?" George tugged at Nellie's apron.

"He's next door, playing with a friend," Nellie said. "But he'll be home soon, and Florence and Paul will be up from their nap, too."

The children marched into the kitchen and headed straight for the box of toys that Nellie kept between the plaid couch and the dining-room doorway.

As Lizzie led her horse into the tree-covered

shed behind the house and tied her to the hitching post, Nellie went outside to meet her mother. Mrs. Mooney was stooped from many years of hard work on the farm, but she walked briskly up the path.

"Now, Nellie, I'm not helpless yet," her mother said as Nellie reached out to take her hand. "I can manage fine." She bristled on past Nellie and up the steps onto the stone stoop at the back of the house.

Nellie walked over to her sister, who still had her apple-blossom complexion and bright brown hair. Lizzie always made Nellie feel better about life.

"I wish you'd come more often," Nellie said.

"I'd like to, but you know how hard it is with the children."

"Yes, when you have three — just like me! I know exactly what you mean."

"How does that poem go — about having three children?"

Nellie thought for a moment, then recited the whole thing by heart:

> "When you have one,
> You can take it and run,
> When you have two,
> Perhaps you can do,
> But when you have three,
> You stay where you be."

Then, with their arms around each other, the two sisters walked up toward the back stoop. Nellie wished for a moment that she and Lizzie could stay outside and leave the children to fend for themselves. It was a warm September day, and out in the field beyond the yard, goldenrod, wild sage, and gaillardia bent in the soft breeze.

But they went on into the house, of course, and there they stopped short. Olive had taken the blue gingham broadcloth from the ironing board and draped it over her shoulders. She was dragging it across the kitchen floor. Nellie looked with horror at what used to be her manuscript. Its pages were scattered in the dining-room doorway and all over the kitchen floor.

"May I have a pencil, Aunt Nellie?" said young George, picking up a sheet. "I'll just put my name on the back of this page. See? There's nothing on the back."

Nellie rushed past Olive, nearly tripping over her gingham "gown." "No, George, that's mine!" she snapped, whisking the manuscript out of his hands.

"Whatever is all that writing?" said Mother, who had enthroned herself in the rocking chair beside the stove. Lizzie glanced sympathetically in Nellie's direction. She seemed to know what it was.

Nellie felt embarrassed. Maybe her work was juvenile as the judge had said. All the same, she wasn't going to act childish about it. "It's a story I entered into a magazine contest — *Colliers'* magazine," she said. "It came back last week. I didn't win, but it did get honourable mention! They called it 'a delightful story with humour and originality.'"

Lizzie grabbed Olive and the trailing yards of blue gingham. She folded the material neatly and put it back on the sewing machine.

"It would be original all right," said Mother. "Remember the time you had most everyone in the neighbourhood believing you'd seen a green wolf? You may even have believed it yourself," she sighed. "You were such a high-strung child. But I would have thought you'd have outgrown such nonsense by now. It isn't as though you don't have enough to do, with a husband and three children."

Nellie grimaced. She did have plenty to do. But surely even a busy mother should have a little time to do something she loved.

George had found Jack's wooden horse on wheels and was pushing it quickly around under the table, barely missing the table's fat wooden legs.

"I just bet you didn't have a chance," Lizzie burst out. "They knew who'd win before they ever began! So don't you fret, Nellie. I do wish you'd read us the story after supper."

"I will sometime . . . but not today," Nellie answered quietly. She didn't agree with Lizzie, but her sister's enthusiastic support made her feel a little better.

Thump. A child had jumped out of bed upstairs. Now the circus would really begin!

Florence and Paul were happily playing train with Lizzie's girls while Jack and George were practising catch with a baseball in the backyard. Lizzie had gone to the general store to pick up a week's groceries and farm supplies. Nellie was up to her elbows in flour, putting together a cake.

Mrs. Mooney sat and rocked by the stove.

"Choo — choo!" shouted Florence. Paul, Olive, and Clara clambered onto chairs or wrapped themselves in the blankets that were draped around the floor. It was a jumble of a train with different passengers facing in different directions. The train also bounced up and down as the restless children waited for it to start.

Knock! Knock!

Who could *that* be? Nellie wondered. She raced to the door. There stood the Reverend Mr. Young, the new minister of the Manitou Methodist Church. He looked a bit lost.

"Come in, Reverend Young. Do come in." Nellie shook his hand with her damp one, then led him over to the rocking chair beside the stove. Her mother had fallen into a light doze and her head had dropped onto her chest. "Mother," she said. Mrs. Mooney raised her head and looked up — a little dazed. "I'd like you to meet our new minister, the Reverend Mr. Young."

Mrs. Mooney became immediately alert and held out her hand. "I'm so pleased to meet you, Reverend Young. I've heard about you and what a fine preacher you are. So nice of you to come to these parts, and us so isolated."

"Thank you, Mrs. Mooney. Those are kind words. I am trying, but it's hard sometimes to find workers in the church. And a man can't do it all by himself."

"That's true. But I'm sure my daughter Nellie here and my son-in-law Wes will be willing to help you in whatever way they can. Isn't that so, Nellie?"

Nellie had just poured milk into the dry ingredients in her bowl and was now frantically trying to beat up the batter. She had to get the roast out of the oven before it burned and this cake batter in, so the cake would be baked in time for dessert. But Nellie smiled at the minister and nodded.

"Bang! Bang! Bang!" yelled all three train passengers as they tumbled out of their train and crashed into each other. A heavier thud followed as all the chairs fell to the floor. The noise surprised even Nellie as she set the roasting pan down on the back of the stove with a hard whack and turned to look at the train wreck.

"Oh, mercy!" said Mrs. Mooney, raising her voice. "Do you children need to make so much racket?"

"Yes," said Florence staunchly. "Our train went in the ditch!"

"Hummmph." Mrs. Mooney looked up at Nellie. "They've inherited your imagination. They don't get this from their father. And, mark my words, you'd better curb them now or they'll have trouble their whole lives." Then she turned to the minister. "Really, I don't know what this generation is coming to. I always saw to it that my young children were seen and not heard."

You did that, all right, Nellie thought. You constantly told me to hush my talk. But I didn't always. And I'll never treat my children that way. She didn't say a word aloud, however. She just turned away and pushed her cake pan into the oven. Closing the door, she drew off her mitts and turned again to the minister, who was still looking at her hesitantly.

"Mrs. McClung, I suppose I shouldn't have called, since you're so busy, but could you possibly lead the Ladies' Aid meeting at the church tonight? I haven't been able to find anyone else or I wouldn't have bothered you. I tried Mrs. Wheeler but she's doing something for the WCTU, and Mrs. Brown is busy with farm work — and they were at the end of my list. I know how busy you are, but . . ."

Nellie smiled and said, "Don't worry. I'd love to do it."

"Why, thank you," the minister said with a sigh of relief. He shook Nellie's hand and her mother's and hurried across the room, stepping over young Paul, and let himself out.

Nellie scooped Paul up and sat down with him on her lap. "Watch where you're going, young man," she said. "You almost got run over by another locomotive."

"Oh, Nellie," her mother said, "you're as senseless as a young child." She rocked back and forth furiously.

"I'm going to the cellar for potatoes," Nellie said, turning to her mother. "Do you suppose you could keep the children away from the cellar steps? It's faster for me that way."

"Certainly." Mrs. Mooney followed her daughter into the pantry, where Nellie pulled up the trapdoor next to the cistern and disappeared down into the darkness.

In a couple of minutes, Nellie reappeared. She set the basket of potatoes down on the floor and closed the trapdoor.

"Now, let me do those, Nellie," Mrs. Mooney said.

Nellie handed her a potato peeler. She hoped

her mother could manage, for she had had a small stroke and could not move about as easily as before. Still, Nellie knew how much her mother wanted to be useful.

At that moment, Jack burst in through the back door. George was not far behind.

"What's the matter, Jack?" Nellie said, reading the expression on her son's face.

"This man —"

"Yes?" Now Nellie was concerned, so she set down her potato peeler and went over to Jack.

"He — There he is!" Jack pointed out the kitchen window.

It was Abe Smith. He'd strayed into the backyard and was snoozing in a hammock under the McClungs' Manitoba maple.

"It's all right, Jack. That's just old Mr. Smith. He won't hurt you. He's just having a sleep under our tree."

"But he shouldn't! It's too near my baseball diamond!"

"Yes, I know, Jack, but he gets mixed up sometimes. Here, you help Grandma. You can pick out the potatoes to peel! And don't you worry about Mr. Smith."

Mrs. Mooney shifted in her chair and glowered at her daughter. "Nellie, let the poor boy recover. And besides, he shouldn't be helping with the potatoes! That's women's work!"

Half an hour later, Nellie turned back to the stove, reached into the oven, and pressed one finger down on the nicely risen cake. As she took the cake to the side cupboard, Wes opened the back door and came inside. Nellie knew it was too early for him to be home.

He staggered across the kitchen, sank onto the couch, and put his head in his hands.

"Whatever is the matter, Wes?" Nellie asked softly.

Wes raised his tired eyes to hers. "I almost . . . I almost . . . killed a horse!"

"You what?"

"Yes. Fred Naismith's prize stallion."

"How could you do that, Wes? I just don't understand." With the arrival of Wes, the children had suddenly gone quiet, and they gathered around now to watch him.

"My assistant, you know the new one, Randolph? Well, he filled a prescription for the horse's drench with boiled — instead of raw — oil. It would have killed him for sure."

"How did you miss catching it?" Nellie gasped.

"Well, I was filling another prescription, and Fred was in a hurry to be off home. So Randolph let him go, saying he'd check with me later. Then Mrs. Ingram came in. She's visiting her sister and couldn't resist coming in and giving me all the gossip." Wes leaned back and seemed to relax a bit. "Anyway, when I finally wrenched myself away from her and checked the prescription, I saw what he'd done. Luckily, George Ingram was right outside and let me ride his mare to go after Randolph.

"I didn't catch him before he got home, but he

hadn't given the horse the drench yet. So I made it in time. I can tell you Fred wasn't too happy, either, when he realized how near his horse had come to a terrible end."

"It's all your fault, Nellie," barked Mrs. Mooney from her powerful position in the rocking chair beside the stove. "Give up this foolishness about writing and take care of your man *properly*. Look at him! He's as thin as a rail fence!"

"Oh, Mother Mooney, it's not Nellie's fault," Wes said. "She's busy with the children all day."

"Well, she's not too busy to waste time writing a worthless novel."

"It's not a novel. It's a *short* story!" Nellie burst out.

Now Wes looked up at Nellie with a puzzled expression. He knew she hadn't planned to tell the family about the contest. "I received my manuscript back — just this morning," she explained. "I didn't win." She turned and walked briskly to the cupboard to see if the cake was cool enough to be iced. As she passed the window, she could see Mrs. Ingram's stout figure and her husband's lean one approaching the back door. She blinked. This day was going from bad to worse to impossible!

"Hurry, Jack," she said, "and you too, George. Be good boys and pick up the chairs for me. Quick! We're going to have more company."

Nellie opened the door just in time for Mrs. Ingram to step inside.

"We've come to see how Wes is," Mrs. Ingram began. "George told me what a ride he had! Poor Wes, I guess the pharmacy business is too much for him. I always said that boy is good at lacrosse, but when it comes to —"

". . . to the pharmacy, he'll do just fine." Mr. Ingram finished his wife's sentence and dug her ribs with his elbow. "Now, we've come to see how you are and to rest our horse. She's a little weary, so we thought we'd stop for a bit before we headed back to Nancy's sister's. They're five miles away."

"I'm glad you've come," said Mrs. Mooney. "Maybe you can talk some sense into my daughter. She's wasting her time writing novels! I've known a few women in my day who had time for reading novels, and they just got addicted. Their families suffered, I can tell you!"

Nellie stabbed a fork into the boiling potatoes. There was no point in arguing. She looked over at Wes, who gave her an encouraging smile. They'd have a good laugh about all of this later. Meanwhile, she had to live through a dinner with Mother *and* the Ingrams.

She opened the cupboard door. Fortunately, her cake had risen nicely. She'd show Mrs. Ingram and Mother what a great meal she could serve — even if she did write stories.

5

"It's beautiful," Nellie exclaimed. She and Wes were exhausted but happy as they stared down at the new Brussels carpet, spread out flat and smooth over the floor of the sitting room. It was a rich, golden tan, covered with wreaths and scrolls. But the main attraction was a bright brown-and-orange-speckled lily in the very centre. It was exotic and wonderful and unlike any lily Nellie had ever seen.

Two months before, she and Wes had measured the room and ordered the carpet from Toronto. This morning, the great bulk had arrived from the train station on a dray cart. Nellie thought they'd never get it to fit in to the corners, but they had, and it looked wonderful.

"Can we come in now, Mama?" Florence ran

through the dining room without waiting for an answer, her brown curls bouncing. It was the middle of June, 1903, and she had turned four in January. Paul was now two and a half, and they had all celebrated Jack's sixth birthday two days before, on June 16. Jack had now completed Junior First Class and passed into Senior First.

"Come now, Florence," Wes said as he scooped the mischievous little girl into his arms. "We have to put the furniture back." He carried the giggling Florence into the kitchen and set her down beside her brother Paul. Then he headed back into the dining room, carrying a pair of maple chairs.

Paul had made a home for himself under an armchair that had been set up against the kitchen couch. He was playing quietly there with a green, toy frog Nellie had sewn out of a scrap of broadcloth — quietly, that is, until Florence arrived.

"I'm a bear," said Florence, "and I eat frogs."

Paul started to cry.

Florence paid no heed and set to work, chewing on one of the unfortunate frog's legs.

"Maaaaa!"

Alice came running from the pantry where she'd been getting ingredients for biscuits. She was rushing to help prepare for the WCTU meeting being held at the McClungs' that night.

"You come with me now, Florence," she said to the feisty four year old. "Don't be pestering your little brother. Your ma and pa are busy. They don't need Paul screeching."

"All right, I'll go and help Mama and Papa, then."

"Don't bother them! Come and help me make biscuits for the meeting tonight."

Florence brightened and was finally persuaded to leave her brother alone.

In the sitting room, Wes surveyed the scene before him. "Our house looks great, Nellie," he said as he put the last chair in place. "And it's amazing — you paid for that rug with money you earned writing ads for the pharmaceutical company!"

"Someday, I hope I can earn enough to pay for more than just a carpet. Then you can sell the drugstore and we can retire." Wes smiled and Nellie continued, "Did you know that you could also sell everything *I* own and keep it for yourself?"

"Yes, I knew that. Any husband in Manitoba can sell his wife's property. So our women need you to fight for them."

"That's true, but I'm also getting worried about *you*. You look so tired these days. Maybe you *should* sell the drugstore."

"I don't think so, Nell. Every job has its drawbacks and — lunch hour is over! I've got to get back to the store." Wes gave Nellie a quick hug and left.

She could hear the screen door close as he went out. Warm June air drifted into the house, and Nellie leaned against the cream-coloured trim between the sitting room and the dining room. She rarely had time to think these days, but she just had to stop for a minute and look over their handiwork. Bright chintz curtains hung beside the long, deep windows and blended with the rich golden brown shades in her rug. Then the shadow of a swallow fell across the new gold-flecked wall-paper.

The house was now almost exactly the way she'd always wanted, from the upstairs to the white-washed cellar. Her linen shelves were neat and her fruit cellar was lined with shelves of preserves. Even the old kitchen couch had been repaired and reupholstered in green-and-white-striped canvas.

Nellie gazed about her with satisfaction. She sniffed the fresh smell of the new paint and carpeting and . . . the distinct odour of . . . something burning in the kitchen!

She reached the kitchen just in time to see Alice taking a pan of charred biscuits from the oven. Smoke billowed toward the ceiling, and Florence set up a wail that could have been heard in Brandon.

"Oh, Mrs. McClung, see what I've done now!" said Alice, looking at Nellie with fear in her hazel eyes.

"Don't you worry about it one little bit."

"But you're in such a hurry today . . ."

"Don't worry, Alice. Just make another batch."

"You're . . . not going to cuff me about the ears?"

"The thought never entered my mind!"

"Back home in England, the cook would've done that right away."

"Well, you're in Canada now — and you're *my* maid-of-all-work. That means I take good care of you."

Later that afternoon, the sitting room and the kitchen were gleaming and the children were having their naps. Nellie was busy preparing snatches of her evening's talk as she threw together two dozen batches of gingersnaps. These, along with Alice's biscuits and the lemon cookies she always had on hand in the cellar, would be ample for the refreshments.

As Nellie sifted flour onto the egg-and-butter paste in the bowl, she thought about all the wonderful women working with her at the WCTU. Since the big meeting in the Town Hall two years before, the Manitou branch had kept in touch with women all over the province. She and Mrs. Nash had begun a lively correspondence, and Mrs. Brown had helped Nellie start up a debating society.

Over at Carman, Mrs. White and the other WCTU women had been battling against liquor licensing in their town. They had had some success, because women other than Mrs. White owned property there, and so were allowed to vote in municipal elections. There must be a lot of widows and single women in Carman, Nellie thought, since a married woman could not own property. On her wedding day, everything a woman owned shifted to her husband's name.

Suddenly, a large crash came from the sitting room.

It was Alice again.

Whatever can have gotten into her today? Nellie wondered.

Alice appeared in the doorway with a downcast face. "Oh, Mrs. McClung, I've . . ."

Nellie wiped her hands on her big-print apron and headed for the sitting room, where Alice had spilled a vase of fresh peonies and tiger lilies —

water and all — right onto the new carpet.

"Is something making you nervous today?" Nellie asked, looking at Alice.

"Oh . . . nothing . . . and everything."

"What is it?"

"It's the weather, I swear. I can feel a bad storm coming."

Nellie nodded. It did seem a little hotter. "But there's something else."

Alice looked down and then looked up at Nellie. "Me ma heard from *her* mother back in England. Grandpa is very sick. He could even be gone by now. We're all feeling badly."

"Maybe your grandma will come and live with you here."

"That's what I said, but Ma says it's too far for her to travel. And I'm sorry about spilling them lilies on the floor."

"Just take a pan of water and clean them up. It's a good thing they spilled right at the edge. There are lots more lilies in the backyard and the carpet's still in perfect shape. I'm sure it will last us many, many years."

"Thank you, ma'am. No use crying over spilt milk, as the sayin' goes."

"No, Alice, there isn't."

Nellie was actually looking forward to giving her speech that evening. As the women of the WCTU crowded into her newly carpeted sitting room, she glanced over her notes one last time. Something nasty had happened in Carman, and it was her job to convince the Manitou women to do something about it. But first, she was going to give them a vision of what the WCTU could be.

"Good evening, Nellie," said Mrs. Brown as she settled into the loveseat in front of the north window. "I hear there've been bad doings at Carman."

"Yes, there have. It will be a topic of discussion tonight!"

Mrs. Brown nodded, her tanned face taking on an unusually serious expression. Her youngest son was sitting at the far end of the loveseat, reading a book he'd brought along.

Mrs. McClung came in the front door next, looking regal in a bright-green silk dress with a fine lace collar and cuffs.

The smell of fresh-brewed coffee was just beginning to waft in from the kitchen as the last woman stepped into the room and found herself a chair. It was Mrs. Ingram. Nellie wondered again why Mrs. Ingram came to the meetings. Perhaps she was acting as some sort of spy. Still, what faster way to spread news about the organization? Mrs. Ingram always told everything to everyone, whether they wanted to hear it or not!

"As many of you are now aware," Nellie began, "the WCTU has begun to expand its work. We do little things and big things — any good work to help a neighbour or a child." Nellie looked over at Mrs. Brown's son. Mrs. Brown could have used some help raising *him* right after her husband died.

"We are best described as organized motherhood, for we have banded together to make life easier and safer for girls and boys. Whatever tries to destroy our homes — whatever hurts our children — whatever makes it harder for anyone to do right — these are our enemies — these we are pledged to fight.

"But WCTU women no longer feel their 'homemaking' efforts lie only within their own four walls. We could work our fingers to the bone, helping other women, teaching children, and fighting the liquor traffic. But we would not be much further ahead. So we must branch out in our efforts." An expectant silence fell over the room. To Nellie's surprise, few women looked shocked. The news of the dispute at Carman must have travelled fast.

"I have just received a telegram from one of our fellow members in Winnipeg — Mrs. Claudia Nash. She has finally succeeded in getting an appointment with Manitoba's premier, Sir Rodmond Roblin, regarding the horrible working conditions in the factories in Winnipeg's North End. This is a perfect example of the type of thing we all must do."

"But Nellie, dear, we can't all talk to the premier," said Mrs. Ingram.

"Of course not, but Mrs. Nash can. She is trying to make life easier and better for people who work in appalling conditions. The politicians have known about the situation for years, but they have done nothing! A woman like Mrs. Nash will begin to change things for the better."

"Well, that's fine, but what do you suppose we can do?"

"There *is* something we can do, Mrs. Ingram,

and it's right at our doorstep. You've all heard of the trouble at Carman?" Nellie turned to the assembled group. A few women looked puzzled, but most nodded their heads. "Well, amazing as it may seem, there are enough women property owners there to sway the vote in the upcoming municipal election against the pro-liquor candidates. As you know, unmarried or widowed women who own property may vote in municipal elections. The WCTU have informed these women of their rights.

"These noble women plan to swing the vote against the liquor interests and eventually deny the hotel owners of Carman their liquor licences."

There were open murmurs of delight from the women. A few of them took notes. Mrs. Ingram shifted a little on her oak chair. The golden light of the spring evening did nothing to soften the harshness of her expression.

Nellie leaned forward and looked straight at Mrs. Ingram. "Unfortunately, however, word of their intention has got out. The Hotelkeepers' Association has appealed to the government of Manitoba — and complained that Carman is being run by women! So the government is going to its advisers."

Nellie's voice had risen to a well-controlled crescendo as she finished. Then she sat down.

"There isn't much they can do, is there?" said young Jennie Gills from her rocking chair. In her arms, she held her youngest child. She had safely delivered this one, her second baby, the last night of the convention two years before. Her husband, outnumbered by the three convention women billeted at her home, had managed to stay sober. But little Jennie was expecting again in late fall. What would happen this time was anybody's guess.

"Well, we can spread the word around that we are in *favour* of the women's action," said Mrs. Ingram. Nellie stared in amazement. Had her mother's friend suddenly swung toward the cause?

"I've heard enough now, coming out to these meetings, and I've seen enough with my own two eyes that I've got to admit it. Some men don't treat women with respect and it's only women that really know it. And besides, over in Carman, what the women are doing is perfectly legal!"

Nellie was so surprised she could hardly think what to say. Her mother-in-law came to the rescue.

"I've always said that all women should have the vote," said Mrs. McClung. "And this incident strengthens that belief. If all women had the vote, the government would not have questioned this situation." Mrs. McClung looked at the women around her with gentle determination. Her beautiful auburn hair, now streaked with white, glowed in the light of the lamp beside her.

"Yes," Nellie said, "and it's up to us to do something. The women of Carman have taken a stand, and we must support them."

"I'll write to the local paper," said one woman.

"I'll bother my local MPP!" said another.

"We'll all work to support the Carman women," said Nellie.

There were murmurs of agreement and a bit of laughter and applause. Nellie felt the group was behind her.

"You made a fine speech, tonight, Nellie," Mrs. Ingram said, looking at Nellie from under the brim of her straw hat. "You know, I've not been sure of your cause until now, but I had a good talk with Mrs. Brown the other day and things began to make a lot of sense. If a widow like her can operate a farm, women can do all sorts of things I never thought they could. And why should women have to make their opinions known through their husbands' votes? Gracious, Mrs. Brown doesn't even have a husband anymore!"

Mrs. Ingram's voice always carried well. Nellie could see Mrs. Brown glancing at the woman and chuckling.

"Well, Mrs. Ingram, I'm so pleased to hear you're behind us. It will be a long road to victory!"

"But a fine one . . . and that's a fine-looking carpet you have — though I wouldn't like to have a big, sprawling flower in the middle of my sitting room. It looks like mud from the Red River when it overflowed its banks."

"Why I adore that lily, Mrs. Ingram," Nellie responded. "And I plan to enjoy it for all the days I live in this house!"

Mrs. Ingram raised her eyebrows and stepped out onto the front verandah.

It was a week after the WCTU meeting, the evening of a stifling-hot day. Until now, June had been fresh and breezy. But the weather had suddenly turned as humid as a midsummer day before a storm. It was eight-thirty and the sun didn't usually set until after ten at this time of the year.

Wes was sitting in the kitchen reading; Nellie was upstairs putting Paul to bed. She softly brushed back the damp hair from Paul's temples. Little rivulets of sweat ran down his face. Jack and Florence were playing in the front yard longer than usual so they could cool down a bit before going to bed.

"You shut up! Don't you dare say Florence's face is dirty!" Jack was shouting at someone.

Nellie leaned out the window and saw two small forms wrestling on the lawn. She ran down the stairs and out the front door.

"Boys! Stop this minute!" she shouted, standing on the porch steps. Her own Jack, and little Ben Mallen, who lived down the street, disentangled themselves and stood up. Ben's shirt was pulled sideways and was smudged with black loam. Jack was glaring at him from behind a shock of tousled blond hair.

"He started it," Ben said, pointing to Jack. "He hit me first."

"Did you hit him first, Jack?"

"Yes, but —"

"Then you apologize right now."

"He's mean. He insulted Florence and he kicked our dog."

"Jack stepped on our dog's *tail*," Ben whined, then turned and ran down the street toward home.

Nellie sat down on the front step with a sigh. Florence came over and dropped into her lap while Jack stood straight and angry in front of her.

"Now, Jack," Nellie continued. "I want you to tell me all about it."

"He said Florence's face is dirty."

Nellie looked down at Florence's face. It *was* dirty. Bits of cookie were streaked across her cheeks, and there were a few mud spots on her chin. In fact, Nellie could not see a clean spot anywhere.

"Well," she said, continuing to stare at Florence.

Before she could say more, Jack burst into a torrent of words. "*I* could tell her that her face is dirty or *you* could tell her, and that would be all right. We would be telling her so she would wash her face. But Ben flung it at her to make little of her."

Nellie looked at Jack with surprise, then pride. His words showed unusual understanding. "And about his dog," he continued. "I stepped on his tail by mistake, but *he* kicked our dog on *purpose.* A dog knows the difference. I did not hurt his feelings, and Ben did."

Nellie reached out for Jack, and the little six year old wiggled over next to her on the front verandah. "I'm proud of you, Jack," she said softly.

They sat quietly together on the front steps as the blistering sun sank and dark clouds raced across the sky. They were large and ominous and edged with black.

Wes appeared in the doorway. "A storm's coming, for sure, Nellie. And it'll be a bad one. Hadn't you better come in now?"

Nellie knew he was right. She scooped Florence up in her arms and taking Jack's hand, she tiptoed across the fine carpet and through to the kitchen.

Nellie washed Florence's face at the basin by

the door while Jack sat on the kitchen couch, waiting his turn. It was then that the wind started to moan and gain force. "I think I'll close the windows," Wes said, hurrying up the steep back stairs two at a time.

As Nellie was throwing the wash water out the back door, she noticed how densely dark the southern sky had become in a very short time. She could not even see the lilac bushes at the back and side of their property, but she could hear the wind lashing them in the darkness.

Back in the kitchen, she felt better. The wind was high, but their home was secure. She pushed the kitchen door closed and looked at Wes, who was sitting with the children on the couch. Little Paul, still sound asleep, was lying in the crook of his arm.

"I think we're in for a bad one, Nellie. Bolt the door. Then blow out that light," said Wes, "and come over here with us."

With that, Nellie's chest tightened. Wes knew storms, and he was talking as if this one would be terrible. Wes feared fire or he would never have asked her to blow out the lamp.

The winds had grown so loud now that Nellie could scarcely hear. She quickly turned down the wick on the lamp and blew into the chimney. The light flickered and went out.

Then she went over to the couch and sat next to Jack and Florence. The little girl was starting to whimper. "Don't worry, Florence," Jack said, patting her on the arm.

"You'll be just fine," said Nellie. "The wind

sounds like a choo-choo train, doesn't it?" But she was not even convincing herself to be calm.

The family sat huddled together as the wind became stronger and darkness cloaked the room.

Lightning streaked across the sky and lit everything in the kitchen for a brief moment. The crash of thunder came less than a second later.

Suddenly a great and mighty gust of wind hit the house. Even in the sheltered southeast corner, where they were huddled, they could feel the walls shake.

Then there was the sound of breaking glass. Nellie jumped up, reached for the dining-room door and opened it.

Lightning brightened the whole room, revealing shattered glass all over the table, chairs, and floor. The brand-new chintz curtains looked like shredded strings blowing back into the room.

Another burst of wind came with more thunder, and the door slammed shut in her face. Nellie grabbed the end of the couch and groped her way back to her family. She put her arms around Florence and held her tight. Jack had crawled into his father's arms next to Paul.

Then came the sound of windows breaking upstairs, and Nellie thought she could hear timber cracking. Was the house going to fall down around them? The storm must have turned into a tornado. She prayed silently for God to protect them. She did not want to pray out loud. The children might feel the fear in her voice.

Paul had wakened and was crying like a newborn. Florence took the cue and began whimpering in earnest. Jack was breathing fast like a hunted deer.

"It'll be all right," Wes said in his strong, kind voice. "We'll be just fine. This kitchen never gets the wind the same as the rest of the house." He reached out for Nellie and Florence, and they huddled even closer together.

Florence and even Paul stopped crying, and Nellie took fresh courage from her husband's strength. They waited for what seemed a long, long time.

Finally, the wind let up somewhat. The lightning came less frequently and the thunder began to sound as if it was farther away. But the rain came down in even heavier torrents.

"The danger has passed," said Wes after a few moments. "It's just a rainstorm now."

Nellie began to relax. It was just a normal summer night again — except for the continuing heat. She set Florence down on the couch. Wes laid Paul beside her. They were fast asleep. But not Jack! "Is it over?" he asked with some disappointment in his voice. "I thought it was going to last all night!"

"Fortunately, the show seems to be over for now!" said Wes. "Why don't you curl up in that rocking chair, Jack? That might help you get to sleep."

Nellie and Wes went into the dining room to look at the damage. Every window was broken, and rain was still coming right inside. Jagged splinters of glass clung to remnants of the shredded curtains. Water bubbled against overturned chairs and over broken flowerpots. Nellie's best books were riding along the little waves. Large sheets of broken glass lay beneath the water and covered much of the carpet, so that the pattern was no longer even visible under the dirt and debris.

They stared in shock at the ruins of their home. "My books! Our beautiful carpet!" said Nellie.

"Yes, I'm afraid it's beyond repair," Wes sighed.

Nellie surveyed the scene in despair. Then she felt Wes's hand tighten over hers and realized how lucky they really were. They still had each other and the children. No one had been hurt.

"I never did like that spotted lily," Wes said the following morning as he and Nellie stared again at the damage.

The lily no longer seemed to matter to Nellie as she picked up a book that was floating by. It was a volume of Charles Dickens given to her by her oldest brother, Will, many years before — when she'd first become a teacher at the age of sixteen. Six years ago, Will had sold his farm to Jack, and moved with his family to Winnipeg, where he now worked as a real estate agent.

"I'm going over to the general store to see if there's any glass left in the place," Wes said. "Then I can start working on those windows. It's going to be another hot day, but that'll help dry things up."

Every window on the north and west sides of the house had been broken, but by mid-morning, Wes had repaired two in the bedrooms and covered the others with thin board taken from packing boxes at his store. Then he headed back to the drugstore. There would be more than the usual number of customers today.

Later that day, as Nellie was preparing supper, she was glad to hear the whistle of the train in the distance. She knew the station agent would have telegraphed Winnipeg for glass and hoped Wes would have time to pick up more. At noon, when he'd hurried home for a sandwich, he'd reported no severe injuries in the area. The storm had hit when most folks were safely home, exhausted from such a stifling-hot day.

As the supper hour approached, Nellie's lack of sleep began to catch up with her. Then, as she looked up from the spider frying pan, where a half-dozen eggs were sizzling in bacon fat, she was surprised to see her brother Jack walking past the window. He came in the back door and stood there without saying a word. Instantly, she knew something terrible was the matter. He was wearing a suit and must have come by train.

"Is it Mother? Whatever is it, Jack?" Nellie asked, her hand still holding the frying pan.

"Mother is fine," he said. "It's Lizzie's husband! Oh, Nellie, he's been hit by lightning."

"But he's going to be all right — he is, isn't he?"

Jack just shook his head.

"Oh, Jack. What happened?"

"He was going after the cattle to bring them

inside before the storm, and the lightning hit him. The doctor says he died instantly."

"Oh, poor Lizzie! And the children!" Nellie started to untie her apron. "We'll get ready to go back with you, Jack. Please . . . go tell Wes."

6

Nellie was walking down Manitou's main street in the bright June sunshine. She was nine months pregnant, and her usual brisk walk had been replaced by something between an amble and a shuffle. The distance between her house and the post office was about all she could handle. She had not told anyone, but this morning, she had felt her first labour pains. She knew that the next McClung would be entering the world any time now — perhaps later today.

Three years had passed, almost to the day, since the disastrous cyclone had hit, and life had returned to normal for everyone except Lizzie. A month after her husband's sudden death, she and Mother had come to stay with Nellie for a while. Lizzie had spent her days staring out the sitting-room window, becoming sadder and sadder, barely eating and not even asking about her children. After the first winter without Tom, Lizzie seemed to brighten as the days lengthened, and gradually she returned to her kind and helpful self. After a year, she was able to talk about the good times she'd had with Tom.

Fortunately, since Lizzie had a clear deed to their good-sized farm, she'd rented out half a section to a nearby farmer and hired an English immigrant to work the other half. Tom and Lizzie had also worked hard and set aside savings. So Lizzie was able to care well enough for her young family. In fact, she was better off financially than some of her neighbours, who held only quarter-sections.

"Hello, Nell!" It was Mrs. Brown, decked out in a pinstriped skirt and a freshly starched blouse. Nellie was about to return the greeting but was distracted by the sight of Abe Smith shambling down the other side of the street. He was sober at the moment, but his clothes looked as if he'd slept in a hayloft. He must have ripped them during his last bender.

"Heading to the post office?" Mrs. Brown asked.

"Why, yes," said Nellie, "and you must be going out to see Lizzie." Mrs. Brown had taken to visiting Nellie's sister, since they were both widows now. In spite of the distance, the tireless Mrs. Brown never let a week go by without paying a visit or sending baking.

"Yes, I'm on my way this very minute. It's good *you're* not going far — not in the condition you're in!"

Nellie smiled graciously, but inwardly wondered at the woman's bluntness. Ah, well, a woman who ran a farm by herself would have to know how to get to the point!

"You'll find piles of letters for you at the post office," said Mrs. Brown. "I've picked up a huge lot myself. The postmaster says they came from that trainload that was delayed when the rails were washed out north of Superior last month. Some of my letters are three months old!"

"Three months! Are they still readable?"

"Oh, yes, but I guess some weren't. Even after they fixed the rails, it took a long time to get to the wreck and retrieve the lost mail — and then sort through it all."

"A terrible disaster," Nellie said and the two women went their separate ways.

When Nellie arrived at the post office, there was already a lineup. She wedged herself through the door and bumped against the side wall as she wiggled into place. It was not easy to navigate when your dimensions kept changing from one day to the next.

"Morning, Nellie," said Mr. Giffen, the postmaster, as Nellie approached the wicket. "Big news for you today — a letter from Ontario, one from Winnipeg, and a few more."

When Nellie looked at the return address on the envelope from Ontario, she kept her conversation as short as possible. Then she hurried back home as quickly as she could, considering she was nine months pregnant *and* going uphill.

The letter with the Winnipeg postmark was

from Mrs. Nash. The one from Ontario had been
sent by the William Briggs Publishing Company in
Toronto — no doubt rejecting her latest revision
of "Sowing Seeds in Danny."

After the *Colliers'* contest, Nellie had sent her
story about Pearlie to one publisher after the other.
But it had been rejected every time. Finally, exactly
one year ago, an acceptance letter had arrived from
E.S. Caswell, an editor at Briggs. He'd said that
while cleaning out his desk one day, he'd found
her manuscript. More importantly, he'd said that
Nellie's story should be a book and asked if she
would like to write more. Since then, Nellie had
spent every spare moment writing and revising
new chapters. Caswell was a very kind and helpful
editor. Whenever Nellie finished a chapter, she
mailed it off to him, and he sent back a lot of
good suggestions about ways to improve it.

"What's in all the letters, Mama?" yelled five-and-
a-half-year-old Paul, who had freed himself from
Alice's grip and run at Nellie's legs like a torpedo.

Nellie pulled the letter out of the envelope as
her brown-haired son began to wind himself up in
the hem of her full skirt, crumpling his new
Buster Brown suit. She tried to stop her hands
from shaking. Why would Caswell send her a letter
without part of the manuscript to work on —
unless he was rejecting the revisions after all? She
unfolded the letter and braced herself for the
worst. After all, publication was not guaranteed,
and Nellie had not been pleased with her last few
chapters. She read silently:

April 26, 1906

Dear Mrs. McClung,

Tonight at home I got my first chance of a good read of this story of yours — and I finished it up. I can hardly describe to you the sensations or emotions it evoked. It is a wonderful story — not a dry one, for humour and pathos alike keep tugging at the tear ducts. I don't know when a story moved me more than did your closing chapters. Well for me I was alone . . . for I discovered how emotional I am as the tears streamed down my face. Those are wonderful chapters, there is a deep well of pathos in them. And yet through my tears I found myself bursting into a chuckle over some of your inimitable touches of humour.

Fortunately, I have been able to persuade our publishing department at Briggs Company to go ahead with publication as soon as we find an American company to help with the expense.

I am most hopeful that you will soon be seeing "Sowing Seeds in Danny" in print.

E.S.C.

Nellie was not one to cry, but her eyes glistened as she read the part about this hard-nosed editor in tears. Then she composed herself and reached down to lead Paul to the stool beside the stove.

"Your mama might just be an author any month now, Paul! What do you think about that?"

"An Arthur, ma'am?" said Alice, staring at Nellie with her eyes open wide. "Like the one with the Knights of the Round Table? I've heard many a tale about him. He was a good and fair king — just like you . . ."

"Not an Arthur, Alice," Nellie grinned. "An author. A writer of books."

"Oh, that's better — not that I didn't like King Arthur."

"Well, Alice, I'm glad you liked the tales about King Arthur, and I hope you'll like my stories too. But isn't it time for your piano lesson?" Alice could now afford piano lessons, for her grandfather had died and left her a little money.

Alice gratefully took off her apron, hung it next to the side table, and collected her music from the piano in the sitting room. In minutes, Nellie had put on her new yellow apron and started peeling potatoes for supper. Out of the corner of her eye, she could see Alice disappearing down the street with little Paul in tow. Mrs. Elliott, the piano teacher, had a son who was about Paul's age, and they always played together while Alice had her lesson. Nellie loved being a mother, but she never refused if a trustworthy person offered to take care of one of her children for a few hours. It was especially helpful this afternoon, for her pains had returned at regular intervals, and she now knew that the baby would be born that day. She wondered if she should call Mrs. Wheeler from across the street, but decided it was too soon yet.

Still gazing out the window, Nellie reconstructed the story of Pearlie and her little brother, Danny. She revelled in the twists of its plot and wondered what changes she might make to improve it. She could even remember some of the exact words. The Watson family — Danny, Pearlie, and the rest — and the pink lady had been joined by a new character, Dr. Barner. He'd add some spice to the story:

Dr. Barner, brilliant, witty, and skilful, had for many years been a victim of intemperance, but being Scottish to the backbone, he never could see how good, pure "Kilmarnock," made in Glasgow, could hurt anyone. He knew that his hand shook, and his brain reeled, and his eyes were bleared; but he never blamed whiskey. He knew that his patients sometimes died while he was enjoying a protracted drunk, but, of course, accidents will happen and a doctor's accidents are soon buried and forgotten.

Then came one of the better scenes of the book: the drunken doctor was greeted in his office by big John Robertson, whose little boy had been cut with the blades of a mower. Try as he might, Robertson had no success in budging the doctor from his drunken stupor — until the doctor's daughter came in and the two of them stuffed him into Robertson's wagon with his medical bag. His daughter knew he would help the boy once he saw him.

True to his daughter's word, the good doctor bandaged the boy and stayed on to care for him for several days. But not long after that triumph, his daughter found him, once more, in the office of the hotel . . . . What were the words? Nellie stopped for a moment. Ah, yes, "a red-faced, senseless, gibbering old man, arguing theology with a brother Scotchman, who was in the same condition of mellow exhilaration."

Nellie looked out the window and thought. She

needed to do more to free people from the grip of drunkenness — and the poverty and beatings that often went with it. Her writing would help, the WCTU would help, but what good would all this do if men in positions of power did nothing? Nellie knew she needed to fight for women to get the vote. And that would be a very hard battle indeed.

The screen door slammed. Nellie's moment of reverie was over. It was Jack, already home from school.

"Where's Florence, Jack? Has she wandered off again?"

"I don't know. But I suppose I'd better go and find her."

"Yes, Jack. Thank you for doing that," Nellie said. She wasn't worried. Florence often stopped to play with one of the neighbour children on her way home from school.

Jack ran out of the house, slamming the screen door.

Nellie went back to her pile of letters. The second one was from her former pupil Sarah Sayers, asking Nellie to drop in at Roland for a visit if she was ever on her way to or from Winnipeg. That won't happen too soon, thought Nellie, not in my condition! But she was grateful for the invitation. Sarah might yet be a force among the women of the WCTU.

The third letter was from Mrs. Nash in Winnipeg.

Dear Nellie, fellow mother and temperance fighter:

How is it that women must always juggle career and family cares? The other day, I was just getting down to work on an article that is to be published on the Women's Page of The Winnipeg Free Press *about working conditions for factory women, as you might imagine. As inspiration began to set in, my oldest son staggered inside with a nail firmly entrenched in the sole of his boot and foot. He'd been playing on the woodpile (terra incognita and interdite) when a nasty board presented itself to his person. You can imagine the yelling.*

Nellie frowned. The scene was all too familiar.

It was days before I got to that article again, but it was worth it. For it inspired me to write yet another letter to our revered premier, Monsieur Roblin, with a request to show him photographs that I've now taken of the poor factory women at work. And, fancy this, he allowed me another meeting! (You remember, he put me off for a year after my first request. Then over the last five years, I've written to him every three months and had only two worthless meetings.)

So I was not surprised when this next meeting proved to be a complete fizzle as well. Once I arrived at the majestic Houses of Parliament, the pompous duck fobbed me off on his assistant, who tried to placate me with tea and biscuits. (He thinks that's how we women spend our time — gossiping and drinking tea.)

Nellie chuckled and felt a bit sorry for the assistant. Mrs. Nash would have been about as easy to deal with as a tiger!

And when Roblin did *appear, can you imagine what he said to me? Do not imagine; it would spoil your dinner.*

I will just tell you. He said, "I hear you've been on a little excursion, Mrs. Nash, and you have pictures to show me. I'd be most delighted to view them at my leisure. Just leave them with my assistant. You women are always so good at the finer touches — the details of life. Who would have thought of a collection of photographs! A splendid notion! We can include them in a display about our fine city."

Well, you can imagine how eager I was to leave those pictures with him. *I'd just as soon leave a henhouse in the care of a fox! I thrust the pictures under his nose, pointed out how thin and ill the women looked, and headed for the exit (with the photos safely tucked under my arm, I might add). Photo excursions! Ha! Tea and biscuits! I've a mind to take* him *on an excursion — right into one of his fine city's rundown factories. I'd like to see what he'd have to say then.*

We need inspiration here in Winnipeg, Nellie. The women at our WCTU are fine and eager, but they are so discouraged by the antics of our premier and his cabinet. Your women at Carman are setting a good example with their plans to vote out the present town councillors who want to keep up the liquor licensing. I'm sure those men are quaking. They don't want clever women exercising their legal rights to set things straight. And, Nellie, you are an inspiration. I only wish that our women could catch some of your vision. Would you grace us with a speech sometime in the spring? Let me know . . .

"Presenting, the amazing Flor!"

Nellie's higher thoughts were interrupted by her eldest son. "I found her for you."

"How did you find her so quickly?"

"I wasn't far away," put in Florence. "We came home together. But Mrs. Wheeler stopped me to ask about you, Mama. I couldn't be rude and ignore her."

Jack grimaced at his sister while Nellie smiled and said, "That's true, Florence." Then Nellie gripped the edge of the kitchen table and bent over against the sudden spasm that had gripped her across the lower stomach. This baby would be coming sooner than she thought!

Just then, the screen door flew back, and in walked Alice with Paul.

"Oh, Mrs. McClung, it's your time!" Alice gasped as she saw Nellie bent over the table. She threw her music books on a chair beside the door and went to the cupboard for the preserving kettles.

"Yes, Alice. Just fill those kettles with water from the well." Then Nellie turned to Jack and Florence. "Take Paul, please, and go to Mrs. Wheeler's. I'm so glad she's home."

The screen door slammed again as Jack and Florence went out, holding Paul by the hand — and Alice came in. She was already carrying a pail full of water.

Nellie took two sticks of hardwood from the woodbox and threw them into the stove. Then she opened the draft in the stovepipe. When Alice came in again with another pail of fresh water, she had the empty kettles sitting ready on the back of the stove. Alice filled them and pushed them up to the front.

"Now, go to Dr. MacCharles and tell him it's

time. Then go for Wes. And, Alice, please hurry."

Alice took one look at Nellie's pale face and said, "Yes, ma'am. I'll hurry." She ran out the door, banging the screen behind her.

Nellie sank onto the kitchen couch with a second spasm. How long had it been since the last pain? she wondered. Not very long.

When this spasm was over, she hurried into the hall and up the stairs. She had to get to her bed.

Shortly after six o'clock, a handsome young stranger came into the world. A few minutes later, the perfect little baby was snuggled up next to Nellie in a white shawl. His regular breathing was sweet to Nellie's ears. This was the picture that met Wes's eyes as he walked into the room. Paul was striding somberly beside his father as if he knew the importance of the occasion.

"Meet your new son, Wes, and your new brother, Paul," said Nellie, her eyes shining with pride.

A wide smile spread across Wes's lined and anxious face. The sun's low rays glinted off his red hair.

"I came as soon as I could, Nell. I didn't think he'd arrive so quickly."

"Nor did I, Wes, but here he is!"

"He? He? Did I hear he?" It was Jack clambering up the stairs and shouting at the top of his lungs. Florence marched into the room behind him.

"Yes, it's a boy. Now there are *three* of you!"

"We sure have you outnumbered now," said

Jack, poking Florence in the ribs.

"I'm going to have broken ribs right this minute if you don't stop poking me."

"All right, you two, you'd better go downstairs and give your mama a chance to rest. You, too, Paul. I'll be down in a minute." The children tumbled out the door, and Wes walked over to Nellie and took her hand. "You're the best-looking mother I've ever seen," he said and kissed her on the forehead.

Later that evening, after Nellie had slept for a few hours, Wes slipped upstairs again with Paul and sat down beside the bed. The new baby, whose name would be Horace Barrie, was sleeping on a down pillow in a little white-and-blue-lined cradle on the other side of the bed.

"You know what, Mama?" said Paul, sitting in Wes's lap, in his now very crumpled Buster Brown suit.

"What, dear?" asked Nellie.

"I told *everybody!! Everybody* in the *world!*"

"You told them *already*? About Horace?"

"Yes! First I went to Mrs. Wheeler and I said, 'It bin a boy,' and then I said, 'If it bin a girl we would a called her Lizzie.' And Mrs. Wheeler gave me a big hug.

"Then I told Mrs. Sharpe and she kissed me, and Mrs. Dale gave me a candy, and Father Duffy said a little prayer."

Wes looked at Nellie and smiled.

"Then I came home to our next-door neighbours and I said, 'Mrs. Smith, it bin a boy!' I was scared of her because she's so grumpy. And you know what she did? She rolled her eyes up to the sky. So I know . . . she was asking God for a baby for their house, too. It must be lonely for her, since she lives there with just that cranky old man, her husband."

"Yes, Paul, maybe she wishes she had a boy like you," said Nellie. And with this assurance, Paul got suddenly very tired and curled up in his father's lap and fell asleep.

"Nellie," said Wes, "my assistant went to the post office this afternoon and picked up a letter that had just come in. Mr. Giffen said you'd picked up the mail, but this one hadn't arrived yet."

Nellie reached for the letter and her heart leapt when she saw the return address. It was another one from Briggs Publishing. E.S. Caswell must have found an American publisher already! She tore open the envelope and began reading out loud.

June 8, 1906

Dear Mrs. McClung,

I regret to inform you that we have lost your manuscript.

"Lost your manuscript!" Nellie stared at Wes in disbelief. "I forgot to tell you . . . I got a letter from Briggs just this morning. They said they were going to publish the book as soon as they found an American publisher! How could they *lose it?*"

"Read the rest of the letter."

"It is somewhere in our offices, I am sure. But we have looked everywhere and cannot find it. As yet, I had

not shown it to an American publisher. So I do not have any other copy. Do you have another copy? I am so sorry that this has happened.

Sincerely,
E.S.C.

"I don't have another copy, Wes. Only bits and pieces."

"I'm sure it'll turn up, Nell. Just you wait and see."

Nellie's heart sank. With a new baby, she had no time to rewrite a whole manuscript. At this rate, she might never have a book published. After all, she was already thirty-three — quite old, she thought, for a first-time author.

"We'll see your book published, Nell," said Wes, gazing at her with his steady blue eyes.

"Yes," said Nellie, feeling reassured. Then she looked over lovingly at the small bundle in the cradle beside her.

"Oh, Wes," she said, turning back to her husband, "far better to lose a manuscript than a baby. God has been good to us today."

7

"Giddyup, Jasper. Gee! Giddyup!"

As much as Nellie described herself as painfully happy in her marriage, there were moments like this that were mostly just painful. She'd thought all the Christmas gifts had been purchased, and here it was the day before Christmas at three o'clock in the afternoon and she was shopping again. Not only shopping, but she had young Horace in tow. Horace was two and a half now and up to all the tricks of the terrible twos. Plus there was a hole in Nellie's boot, and a big clump of snow had slipped inside it. She was also feeling a bit guilty because she'd overspent on the Christmas presents already — and had yet to buy something for Wes.

She stopped outside the dry goods store next to

the general store, tied Jasper to the hitching post, and put a blanket over him. Then she lifted Horace down from the cutter. She'd seen a wool cardigan inside that she knew would fit Wes perfectly. It was a bit expensive, but she had not had time to knit one, nor did she have time to look for anything else. Besides, Wes was making a decent living now, so she could afford it.

"You're a late shopper, Mrs. McClung. Too busy making speeches, eh?" said Mr. Gardiner, the store owner.

"Horace, why don't you tell Mr. Gardiner about the cutter ride you just had?" Nellie said. She had no patience for people who quibbled about her political work. She knew she could count on Horace to talk the man's ear off until she found the cardigan.

She was relieved to see that it was still on the shelf beside the hats. It was a fine cashmere in rich golden brown — a colour that suited Wes very well.

"I'll take this cardigan, please, Mr. Gardiner," she said. "And would you put it in the nicest box? It's for Wes."

"I'll try to do that." Mr. Gardiner leaned under the countertop and rummaged around.

"I do miss your wife at our WCTU meetings."

Mr. Gardiner emerged from under the counter, coughed, and rang up the sale on his cash register. He was well-known in the town for preventing his wife from participating in any WCTU activities and for being opposed to women's votes.

As he handed Nellie the parcel in silence, she

said, "I'll look forward to seeing your wife at the January meeting. Merry Christmas, Mr. Gardiner."

He nodded his head stiffly in farewell.

Nellie hurried outside. The wind was biting cold, and a thick, lead-coloured sky shaded down to inky blue at the western horizon. Now that she was not so intent on her gift-buying, Nellie noticed that there were other last-minute shoppers out on the street. Mrs. Wheeler was dashing into the hardware store with her husband. Jennie Gills was moving slowly along the board sidewalk on the other side of the street, her head bent against the gusts of snow. She was pregnant again and had three children in tow. They stumbled along like hedgehogs in the fading light of the late-afternoon sun. Abe Smith was marching briskly over to the confectionery in a new set of clothes. He'd stayed sober for a month or so now. Nellie hoped he'd make it through the New Year's celebrations.

Nellie put Horace and her parcel into the cutter, then took Jasper's blanket off, untied him, and clambered up herself. Wes would be home in two hours, and she wanted to finish a few tasks before he arrived. His mother would be spending the first part of Christmas Day with them, and Nellie wanted the house to be spotless. Jasper sped along the short distance to home.

"Come on out of the cold, ma'am," said Alice, holding the kitchen door open as Nellie strode across the back verandah. Alice had a cold herself and was feeling homesick for the big family of cousins, aunts, and uncles who always visited her grandmother's home in England at this time of year. The weather in Canada did not help. Although she had come to love Manitoba, Alice still did not like the winters. The snow and the cold were excessive, in her view. But stalwart as ever, she'd made sure that the Klondike heaters were gorged with wood and was diligently tending the one near the dining room.

"Could you take Horace up for his afternoon nap, Alice? I have a few things I want to arrange in the sitting room." Nellie set her red fox muff and hat on the rack beside the door and unfastened her high black boots. She left her raccoon coat to drip beside the stove.

Then it was into the sitting room to wrap Wes's present before he came home. As she walked into the room, she was dazzled by the sight before her eyes. Nellie had planned it all, but Alice had been busy while she'd been out.

The dining-room table was laid with her mother's Irish linen and her own best blue-willow china. The sideboard was festooned with pine branches and red bows, and a plump but graceful Christmas tree stood at the north end of the sitting room. Wes had cut the tree down on Lizzie's farm. And last, but far from least, was the gleaming red cover of the book that lay on an oak side table next to the tree.

A year after Nellie's manuscript had been lost, E.S. Caswell had found it. He had then contacted an American publisher — Doubleday Page & Company — and now the manuscript was a real book. Nellie had even been able to contribute to the household income from her advance money.

She gazed down at *Sowing Seeds in Danny*, her heart bursting with pride. On the cover was a photograph of a small boy in high black boots, loose long pants, and a big overshirt stretching down to his knees. At the very top, in black print, the title and author's name stood out clearly:

SOWING SEEDS *in* DANNY
by
Nellie L. McClung

Nellie remembered what E.S. Caswell had written when he'd first accepted the manuscript, and glowed again as she'd done then. The Watson family were "real people," he'd said, and he wanted to "know more of them. You could go ahead with this," he'd written, "and make it into a book." And now here it was, at last.

And two days ago, she'd had yet another pleasant surprise from the publisher. She'd told Wes about it, but she was waiting till Christmas Day to tell everyone else.

Nellie snapped out of her daydream and began to wrap Wes's cardigan. She was sure he would love it. Earlier in the week, she'd bought herself a red velvet jacket, since she'd accidentally burned her favourite one while ironing. She knew it didn't pay to write while cooking and ironing, but it was the only time she had.

As she was putting her husband's gift under the tree, she heard the door open. She turned around and saw Wes standing in the doorway, his face ruddy from the frozen air and his eyes shining with joy.

"Is it the fair Nellie Mooney I see before me?" he said with a half-grin.

"Yes, sir, it is the same."

"And would she have room on her dance card for a weary pharmacist tonight?"

"Why, Sir Pharmacist, I have room for no other."

Wes strode across the room, swept Nellie off her feet, and turned her around three times.

"Come on, Sparrow Shins, show 'em what you can do!"

"I'm no Sparrow Shins anymore, Wes, and you know it! But here we go!" And Nellie started into the steps of the "Fisher's Hornpipe" as her Irish father had taught her so many years before. Wes clapped, then stepped in time with her until they were both out of breath.

"Say, Nell," said Wes after a big, long hug, "there are a lot of presents under our tree this year."

"Yes, I'm afraid I overbought a bit."

"*Nellie . . .*"

"Just a bit. We're not poor anymore, Wes. And I didn't really buy that much."

"You kept the bills."

"Most of them."

"Nellie. How many times do we have to go through this? I give you money to run the house, and you, in return, keep records of what you spend. I'm not even asking for a budget — just records, Nellie. You must look after these things more carefully."

"Oh, Wes . . ."

"An intelligent woman like you, and you still can't balance your books!"

"But, Wes, it just bores me. Why don't you do it — or get somebody else to do it? Besides, you shouldn't talk about overspending! I can hardly turn around in the pantry for fear of being knocked on the head by a cured ham. I've never known a man to put away so much meat!"

"Well, one man's meat is another man's poison, that's all I can say!"

And with that they both burst into laughter.

"Oh, Wes," Nellie enthused, "I'd rather quarrel with you than agree with anyone else. You're a fair fighter!"

Nellie gazed at Wes and thanked God for him. And tonight, he looked happy. The pharmacy business was not quite right for him; they both knew it. He worked long hours and often came home looking drained. But tonight was Christmas Eve, and all the cares of the workaday world were forgotten.

"Joy to the world! The Lord is come;
Let earth receive her King;
Let ev'ry heart prepare Him room
And Heav'n and nature sing,
And Heav'n and nature sing,
And Heav'n, and Heav'n and nature sing."

Outside, the winds lashed mercilessly at the walls of the white clapboard house, but inside, the McClungs were as warm as anyone could be at the beginning of a Manitoba Christmas dinner. Long lines of freshly strung popcorn were draped over the branches of the Christmas tree, and a few candles — placed above Horace's reach — were twinkling near the top. The family was seated around a linen-draped oak dining-room table.

Nellie was resplendent in her red jacket, and Wes was wearing the new cardigan Nellie had bought for him the day before. Mrs. McClung was neatly elegant in a green wool dress with brown accessories. Alice had put red ribbons in her light brown hair and was cheerful in spite of her home-sickness.

When they got to the part about nature singing, Horace took it as a signal to jump onto Alice's lap and blow his new tin whistle into her ear.

"Horace!" Alice gasped.

"Come over here, Horace," Nellie said, and plunked her youngest son down into his wooden high chair.

Plates full of turkey and dressing, fringed with cranberry sauce and bubbling brown gravy over creamed potatoes and steaming carrots, were handed round. And soon the fine blue-willow dishes were being sent to Wes for refills at the head of the table.

The three older children were finishing up the last bits of Christmas pudding when Mrs. McClung made an announcement. "I want to tell you, Florence — and Jack and Paul — that you have a very clever mother. She has written such an interesting book that everyone, absolutely everyone, is talking about it!"

"Oh, Mrs. McClung, what have you heard?" Nellie burst out. She sometimes felt like a young girl around her mother-in-law and was prone to say the first thing that came into her mind.

"Nellie, you would not believe the things I overheard on the train from Winnipeg! One man said, 'You know, that book makes me glad I'm human!' And another passenger took a look at his copy and said, 'Why, this is my country. Someone's talking about what I know!' And here's the *pièce de résistance!*"

With that, Nellie's mother-in-law took a letter out of the black purse she had set neatly beside her plate, brushed an insolent crumb off her green bodice, and began to read. "It's from my husband, Nellie. He does so wish he could have been here, but he's terribly busy. Our congregation in Winnipeg is really quite large, and Christmas is such a time for emergencies. But he managed to write a few lines for me to read to you."

Nellie smiled, "I understand, Mrs. McClung. And I'm dying to hear what he has to say." Nellie was a little uneasy, however, for she remembered that her Methodist father-in-law belonged to the old school of thought — and some of the old Methodists frowned on a lot of things — including novels!

Mrs. McClung read: *"I am just finishing* Danny *for the second time, and my opinion of the book has been greatly elevated. So far as my knowledge goes, Pearlie, the main character, is the finest in modern fiction and it's because of her Christlikeness. My dear daughter, never let this quality be wanting in your books and stories when it comes in as naturally as in* Danny."

Tears welled up in Nellie's eyes and started to run down her face.

"My dear, whatever is the matter?" Mrs. McClung spoke with motherly concern.

"His words — they're so kind. May I keep the note?" Nellie reached for the paper and Mrs. McClung handed it to her with a kind smile.

Nellie wiped the tears from her eyes with a handkerchief and started pouring second rounds of tea.

"I wonder what Reverend Young would think about that," said Jack, sounding wiser than his years.

"What do you *think* he would think?" asked Wes, helping himself to a couple of shortbreads.

"Well, Grandpa said Pearlie is Christlike, but Reverend Young said Christlike people should be weak."

"Weak?"

"I guess he meant you had to let people trample over you like a herd of buffalo."

"No, Jack, I think he said *meek* — that means being patient even when it's difficult!"

"Oh, but Pearlie goes around bothering people in Mother's book and trying to make them change. Is that Christlike?"

"Sometimes it is," said Wes. "The worst fault people found with Jesus was that He annoyed them. Even now new ideas blow across some souls like a cold draught, and people naturally get up and shut the door. They have even been known to slam it!"

"Are they going to slam the door on you, Mother?" Jack asked, looking worried.

"Some people might, but if they do, they'll be missing out on a chance to make the world a better place."

"That's right!" Jack said, looking happier. "You show 'em, Mother!"

"Your mother's already shown people a thing or two," said Mrs. McClung. "When I was down in Ontario a few months ago, people there were already talking about *Danny*. And you'd be surprised, Nellie, at how many people want to meet you in person."

"Really?" Nellie was truly surprised to hear this.

"Yes, they do. And, Nellie, I have a special favour to ask."

Nellie looked cautiously at her mother-in-law. It was always hard to say no to her — in fact, nearly impossible. *She* had the convincing way of the meek — the terrible meek — who win by sweetness and gentle persuasion.

"I am trying to raise money for the WCTU's Home for Friendless Girls in Winnipeg. It's called the Willard Home. We badly need money."

"I'm sorry . . . . We live within something of a budget, even though the store is doing well." Nellie heard a stifled cough coming from Wes's end of the table. For a split second, Nellie wondered if Wes was ill. Then she realized he was probably trying not to burst out laughing at the thought of her keeping close track of the household accounts.

Nellie turned back to her mother-in-law. "We'll be doing better once my royalty cheques come in," she said, "but I haven't received any yet — just the advance, and that's been spent. The publisher tells me they generally take a loss on books from first-time writers. But I could get together a few dollars — maybe five dollars from my household budget. Would that be enough?" After all her Christmas shopping, Nellie felt somewhat guilty, but on that particular day they really could not give more.

"No, Nellie! That's not what I'm talking about. I want you to give readings from *Danny* in Winnipeg. The WCTU will rent the hall and charge admission. I'm certain that many people will come."

"Oh, I couldn't. I'm not a speaker . . . and not a real author . . . not like . . . well, say, Ralph C. Connor. Maybe you could ask him!"

"But, dear, you are an author."

"Yes, Mama, you're a *real* author," Jack said.

"Now, don't you worry about the details, Nellie," Mrs. McClung continued, like a duck swimming in familiar waters. "All you have to do is come and read to us. I know folks will come."

"And pay money to hear me? I can't believe it!"

"Everyone loves your book."

"Not everyone."

"*Who* doesn't? I haven't heard of anyone who doesn't like it."

Nellie sat in silence, then she decided to say it outright: "My mother has visited three times since *Danny* was published, and she has never once mentioned the book."

"Are you sure she knew it was published?"

"Oh, yes, I went over by train to give her a copy, the day after it came out. And I also dedicated it to her."

"Never mind, Nellie. Sometimes, people — women, in particular — grow up believing that life is a certain way and that it should never be changed. Then after a while, they *can't* change."

"But you did."

"I've been in a better position to relieve women's suffering. Your mother helped people through sickness and misfortune but could do nothing to improve their situation. She has not seen the bigger world, and maybe she just can't learn new ways now. But I'm sorry, Nellie. It truly is a beautiful book."

"Yes, it's a beautiful book by a beautiful author," said Wes, beaming at his wife. "And I think Nellie has something else to tell us."

"Oh, Wes, you wouldn't let dinner pass without mentioning it, would you!"

"Not on your life. It's your surprise!"

"Well, all right, folks. Here it is." Nellie reached over to the red-ribboned sideboard and pulled open the top right drawer.

Inside was a special edition of *Sowing Seeds in Danny*, bound in soft, natural, buckskin leather, and beside it was a letter from the publisher. Nellie stroked the beautiful, smooth cover with the fingers of her right hand and then held it up for the family to see.

"Mr. Caswell at the publishing house sent me this the other day," Nellie said. "It's our very own edition of *Danny* — and it came just in time for Christmas!"

"Look, Mama, your name's on the front in gold!" Paul exclaimed.

"Yes, and on the inside, it's just as good. It says: To the Author, with the respect and congratulations of the publishers, Toronto, 1908."

"Why would they say that?" asked Jack, biting into a mincemeat tart.

"They said that, and they printed this copy just for me and the family, because —"

". . . you did so much work writing it!" said Florence.

"Partly . . . but also because *Danny* was first on the Canadian bestseller list last month! Here's what the publisher said:

Dec. 10, 1908

Dear Mrs. McClung,

Congratulations! As you can see from the enclosed newspaper, Danny *occupied first place on the bestseller list in Canada last month.*

We at William Briggs and Company are all very pleased. Thomas Allen sends his congratulations on the great success of your book. A handsome royalty cheque will be in the next mail to you.

Once again my sincere congratulations! I always knew you could do it. Have you started the sequel yet? I am waiting impatiently for it.

Sincerely,
E.C.S.

"Here's to our Nell," Wes smiled, holding up a glass of grape juice.

"To our Nell!" The family rose in unison and

drank a toast to Nellie.

"Well, now," said Wes, after everyone had settled down, "let's clean up these dishes. Then I'm going out for a walk, if the storm has eased up enough."

"It is a political scandal of major proportions, Nell," Mrs. McClung said in her usual even tone. She and Wes and Nellie had finished the dishes, and the two women were now warming themselves up with tea in the sitting room. Alice had gone to spend the rest of Christmas Day at her parents' farm, the younger children were playing in the dining room, and Jack was sitting next to the Christmas tree reading *Wild Animals I Have Known*. On the other side of the tree was a beautiful still life of a Manitoba harvest that Mrs. McClung had painted herself. It was a gift for the whole family.

"They crossed the names off the list!" exclaimed Nellie.

"More or less. The Conservatives passed an order in council denying the vote to all the women of Carman."

"That's not democratic! It's a terrible infringement of rights!"

"Orders in council are part of the democratic process, but they are easily abused."

"What are they going to do about it?" asked Nellie.

"What are *we* going to do about it? That's what we should be asking. This affects all women in Manitoba — and Canada, for that matter!"

Nellie stared at Mrs. McClung, her face frozen in shock. Carman was the only place in the whole province where enough women were property owners to sway the vote against the liquor interests in the municipal election. And even there, they had lost!

Nellie had barely let the news sink in when Wes appeared at the dining-room door — earlier than expected.

"Nellie?"

"What's the matter, Wes?"

She rose quickly from her chair and brushed past the tree and the red bows and pine branches on the sideboard. Wes's eyes looked more grey than blue. His shoulders were stooped, and he had forgotten to take off his overcoat.

"It's the store . . . I . . ." he began.

"Wes?"

"Everything's frozen . . . I . . . I shut the door last night — but not tightly enough. It blew open in the storm and everything froze. They're wasted. All the drugs. Wasted."

PART TWO

The Battle

8

A brisk April breeze caught at the pheasant feathers on Nellie's bright blue felt hat as she marched up to the wicket at the Winnipeg train station. She was in the capital city to give a speech at the WCTU. *Come as soon as you can,* Mrs. Nash had written right after Christmas. *We need your voice on the Carman scandal.*

Nellie had sent a letter back that very day to accept the invitation. *I'm going to Winnipeg on January 20th to do a reading from* Danny *at the Willard Home for Friendless Girls,* she wrote. *But I won't have time to give another speech then. Could I come later in the year? I'm willing to do everything in my power to have this scandal exposed. Why don't you come to my reading and we'll make firm plans then?*

They'd agreed that Nellie would return to

Winnipeg in April and spend two days there. That meant four days away from the children — including travelling time and a stop-off at Roland to visit Sarah Sayers. Nellie was worried about being away from home for so many days. But she knew the children would be well cared for, since Alice was now working as a full-time maid and babysitter.

Earlier that morning, Nellie had taken out the soft-blue dress she'd bought for the occasion and packed it into her valise. She wanted to look her very best because there was nothing like a new dress to smooth over the rough patches in a speech. Mrs. Nash had also promised to take Nellie to one of the better hairdressers in Winnipeg. That would help, too.

Nellie had composed the last part of her talk on the train as it travelled past the farms north of Manitou. The cattle were out in the fields now, sampling the first spring grasses. Blue anemones were visible beneath the leafless birches and poplars, and the sun's rays were getting stronger. Most of the farms and small towns between Manitou and Winnipeg were neat and well kept. But there were also untidy little places with broken verandahs and sagging roofs, surrounded by old cans and piles of discarded machinery.

There was no reason for such squalor in a country like this, Nellie thought, where God had made ample provision for everyone. But with governments like Roblin's, the gap between the rich and the poor, between the powerful and the powerless, was growing bigger all the time. The Carman scandal was only one more ploy to keep power in the hands of the wealthy liquor interests and their government supporters. The more she thought about Roblin's dirty trick, the more dramatic her speech became.

Nellie was still thinking about her speech as she stood in front of the wicket, waiting for the ticket agent to notice her. The station clock ticked on as Nellie kept waiting and the ticket agent kept shuffling papers.

My talk may be well-planned, Nellie fumed to herself, but I'll never deliver it at this rate.

"May I help you?" the agent finally drawled, slowly pulling a pencil from behind his ear.

"Yes, you may be able to do that," Nellie said. She set her valise down and opened a large envelope she was carrying. "I purchased this insurance policy at Manitou along with my return ticket. I've just had time on the train to read it."

The man peered past Nellie to the line of people behind her. "I'm afraid I can't answer any of your questions, ma'am. I only sell tickets."

"And insurance? Don't you sell your customers insurance policies here in Winnipeg, too?"

"Well, yes . . . but I don't make up the forms or the rules."

"Who does?"

"I don't rightly know who makes them up."

"Well, may I please speak to your manager?"

"Yes, ma'am, he'll be back from lunch soon."

"I'll wait," Nellie said. She moved out of line and stood watching as the people behind her moved up to the wicket. A quarter-hour passed before she observed a balding man walk up to the ticket counter. He pushed the low swinging door beside the wicket and walked inside. Nellie jumped up at once and caught the door with her hand.

"Are you the manager?" she asked the man's back as he moved toward a desk in the far corner of the room. The man turned and stared at her in silence. "I'd like to speak with you. It won't take long," Nellie said.

"Very well," the man said. "Come in." He sat down at his desk and stared up at Nellie. "Now, what can I do for you?" His voice became more congenial as he took in the trim figure in the fine suit.

Once again, Nellie set down her valise and opened the large envelope in her hand. "For two and a half dollars, I bought this Accident Insurance Policy at the station in Manitou to insure me for five thousand dollars on my trip to Winnipeg and back."

"So what's the problem, lady? I see you're not needin' to collect," the man laughed.

"I read this policy on the way into Winnipeg. And I saw some strange things. It says that 'if the insured be a male' the accident insurance will cover a case of total disability, partial disability, the loss of a hand or a foot or an eye. But a clause on the back says that 'females are insured against death only.'"

"Yes, that's the way it is."

"Why is it," Nellie asked, "that you take a woman's money and give her lower protection than you give a man?"

"Don't you know," the man said severely, "that

women are much more highly sensitized than men, and would be more easily hurt in an accident? They would be victims of pure nerves, and many a woman, particularly not a wage-earning woman, would like nothing better than to lie in bed for a week or two and draw her seven-fifty a week. They would think they were hurt when they really were not, and there would be no end of trouble."

"But, Mr. . . . "

"McGregor's my name."

"Mr. McGregor, what about the clause relating to the loss of a hand or a foot? You would not be altogether dependent on the woman's testimony in that, would you? You could check to see if they were pretending, could you not?"

"Really, I don't have any more time for foolish questions," Mr. McGregor said, putting on his glasses and looking at a pile of papers on his desk.

"Thank you for the information," Nellie said. "I hope to have the opportunity to bring this matter before the next convention of insurance men."

Mr. McGregor looked up quickly. "And have these men asked you to speak to them?"

"No, but they will." Nellie turned abruptly, leaving Mr. McGregor staring after her.

Nellie's cheeks were flushed as she walked out of the train station into the April sunlight on Main Street. She sighed with relief when she saw that Mrs. Nash had already arrived and was waiting for her, standing next to a chauffeur-driven Oldsmobile. The busy city street was filled with horse-drawn carriages. Mrs. Nash's Oldsmobile was one of the few cars in sight. Nellie was not too surprised to see that Claudia owned a car. Her husband was a very successful businessman.

Mrs. Nash's full navy-blue skirt flared out below a brown mink cape. A matching mink hat was perched jauntily on her head, and a royal blue scarf was draped around her neck.

"You look as if you've been in a heated discussion," said Mrs. Nash, taking Nellie's arm and directing her to the car. "Did you buttonhole a poor, unsuspecting opponent on the train?"

"No, a poor, unsuspecting ticket agent and his manager!"

"Tell us everything, right from the beginning. I mean *us*, by the way. I'd like you to meet Lillian Thomas. I've told you so much about each other."

A tall woman with a steady gaze and a calm manner stepped out of the car and shook Nellie's hand. She was wearing a long, plum-coloured coat and a red felt hat with a wide brim covered with clusters of bright imitation wintergreen berries.

"Good afternoon, Nellie. I hear congratulations are in order."

"Congratulations?"

"Yes, on the sale of your book! The bestseller of the year — and the top Canadian seller to date!"

"I'm as surprised as anyone about that," said Nellie, as the three women piled into the back seat of the car. The chauffeur honked at a small boy selling newspapers and pulled out into the street.

"Did you know you're only the second person in the country to write a Canadian bestseller?"

"Yes . . . I share that honour with Ralph C. Connor now. It hasn't really sunk in. And I'm astonished at the number of speaking engagements I have."

"I'm not too surprised," said Mrs. Nash. "I knew you'd be in demand the very first minute I heard you speak — that day in Manitou."

"I do enjoy it, but it makes life very busy — travelling and working on my sequel to *Danny*."

"How can you do both?"

"Well, the income from my book has made it possible for me to hire Alice full-time. And the children are growing older. Horace, my youngest, is almost three."

"I'll be covering your speech this evening for *The Winnipeg Free Press*," said Lillian. "Can you give me some highlights ahead of time?" She took a pen and pad out of her black leather purse.

"Why, yes," said Nellie. "I learned in my research that female property owners have had the right to vote in municipal elections since 1887 — for twenty-two years."

"A longstanding right!"

"Yes, and since 1890, women have had the right to elect school trustees and sit on school boards."

"About twenty years ago, too," said Lillian, scratching her right temple with her pen. "Interesting coincidence. It's also been about twenty years since women in Manitoba really fought for a fair deal."

"Yes," Mrs. Nash interrupted. "There have been few changes in women's favour since those laws went through. Women in Manitoba have become passive. And people find it strange that we're now speaking up for ourselves!"

"Mrs. Nash and I spent a day staffing a table on women's votes at the Winnipeg Stampede two weeks ago and people of all ages were pointing at us as if we were dinosaurs in the flesh!"

"They see us as man haters," said Lillian. "But that's simply not true. Some of our most faithful helpers are men."

"But there are still a good number who refuse to see the light," said Mrs. Nash. "One man saw me at the intersection of Portage and Main yesterday and said to his daughter, 'There's Mrs. Nash, the raging bull!'"

"A passion for justice never was popular," Nellie laughed. "From what you've told me, I wish that man could see the slums of Winnipeg's North End. Then he might understand."

"Well," said Mrs. Nash, "we needn't worry. We're in sight of the Promised Land. It's only a matter of time. But we must refuse to submit to injustice."

"Yes, we will never bow to oppression. In the eyes of God, that would be the same as supporting it," said Nellie.

"I hope that's going to be part of the speech tonight," said Lillian, closing her notepad. "Unfortunately, I can't continue our conversation now. Mrs. Nash's driver is dropping me off in the next block — at the offices of the *Free Press*. But I wanted to meet you before you were surrounded by well-wishers — and it's been a pleasure."

Mrs. Nash and Nellie drove on for a few more blocks to the hairdressing salon where Nellie had an appointment. They emerged into April sunshine while the chauffeur waited in the Oldsmobile.

"I'll just introduce you to the hairdresser — her name's Gertie. And then, unfortunately, I have to dash off to organize this evening's meeting. I'm sure Gertie will do a fine job. She talks a blue streak — but you'll be able to hold your own! And I'll be back to pick you up in an hour and a half."

"So good to meet you, Mrs. McClung," a woman gushed as Nellie and Claudia Nash headed into the salon. This must be Gertie, thought Nellie. "Mrs. Nash has told me *all* about you. And I'm *so honoured* to have the *privilege* of setting your hair. I understand you'll be speaking this evening. I'll do you up grand. You'll be so beautiful you won't even know yourself when I finish."

Nellie tried hard not to laugh. The woman was full of goodwill and had not meant to insult her. "Well, I'm not expecting miracles," she managed to say. "But a wash and a hairdo will help. The CPR runs some very grimy trains."

"Well, that's no problem," Gertie blundered on. "As I said before, you won't know yourself when I'm finished with you. Just come right over to the washbasin." She pointed to a marble basin standing in front of a large, gilt-edged mirror.

Mrs. Nash smiled at Nellie and slipped out the door. "Mrs. Nash is one of my favourite clients," Gertie enthused, "but she's so busy. Spends too much time fighting for women's rights. Not that it isn't a good idea. But what about her family? Do you know what I mean?" Gertie wrapped a fresh white towel around Nellie's shoulders. "Lean back, please, over the sink," she said. Then she pulled the pins from Nellie's hair and started to pour dipperful of water over her head.

"It's a busy time of year or I'd come and hear you talk. I work every weekend, though not Sundays. Of course, nothing is open on Sunday. But I work most of the other days. Sometimes, though, I don't work on Mondays. It all depends. If they want me to come in, I do. I have five kids and my husband is off work in the winters, most of the time. He's a carpenter, you see. And they don't build too many houses in the winters. It being so cold. So I always say to them here, if they want me to come, I will. I could work seven days a week. Actually, I don't mind. Sometimes it's more peaceful here than it is at home . . ."

Nellie tried to say something, but Gertie kept barrelling on. After attempting to interrupt a few more times, Nellie resigned herself to listening. The one-way conversation was mostly about the antics of Gertie's six year old, who was in his first year of school.

A little over an hour later, as Gertie wrapped the last lock of Nellie's hair around a curling iron, she suddenly seemed to remember that she had a famous author in the chair. "Well!" she said. "For the love of Pete, here I am talking all about myself, when you're the one who should be talking, you being a writer and all. I haven't read your book, but I hear it's a delightful story. I'm going to read it someday — if I ever get time. And you know, I've thought about writing myself. Not now, of course, but when I'm old, when I'm too old to do anything else. Well, enough about writing. Take a look at yourself!"

Gertie may have been a dreadful talker, but she was also a hairdressing genius. And she'd put rouge on Nellie's cheeks to tone up her complexion. That was a new item, but it worked a lot better than what Nellie was accustomed to using — the rose-leaf from a summer hat!

As the women of the Winnipeg WCTU rustled into the main hall, the air buzzed with excitement, and light perfumes mixed with the smell of fresh coffee. Nellie was on stage, seated next to Mrs. Nash, trying to remain calm. She had never spoken to such a large group before. She was also feeling pangs of fear and worry about her family. When she'd left Manitou very early that morning, Wes had looked even paler and more drawn than usual. The bronchitis he'd recovered from in March was coming back. And Florence and Paul had been having a fight. Both of them wanted to take last night's potato peelings to Jane Gee, the neighbour's cow, but they didn't want to go together. The issue had still not been resolved when Nellie left for the train station.

Nellie pushed these thoughts out of her mind and gazed at the women in front of her. Among them was Mrs. McClung, right in the front row. She'd promised to be there. And there was Jonas

Babcock, the Conservative MPP Mrs. Nash had described in her letters, who was against women's rights. Lillian had introduced him to her during the dinner. Nellie could not understand why he would want to come and hear her speak. He was a spy, no doubt. Well, she would give him something to talk about!

Applause went up from the assembled crowd, and Nellie stepped up to the podium.

"As I was coming into Winnipeg this morning, I looked out over the countryside and saw farms of two types: there were the well-kept, prosperous ones, and there were the others — surrounded by signs of poverty and despair. What does this have to do with the plight of women in Manitoba today? Surprisingly, a lot. Those prosperous farms were built on the backs of women who worked as hard as, or harder than, the men. The neglected ones — in 90 percent of cases — have fallen victim to the drinking of irresponsible husbands and fathers who would rather drown in whiskey than make sure their children have warm clothes for winter.

"The drinking habits of men in this province have done more to cause misery and poverty than any of us care to think! And, sad to say, it is women who bear the brunt of this misfortune.

"We have, in this province, a premier who prides himself on his chivalry toward women. But is it chivalrous to leave women and children unprotected and subject to the violence of foolish men? No, it is not." And here Nellie looked straight at Mr. Babcock. "Mr. Roblin does not know the meaning of true chivalry.

"Instead of caring for the poor, the widows, and the well-being of this province, Mr. Roblin's Conservative Party has become expert at all kinds of political manipulation. And what has been done to stop this behaviour?"

"Nothing!" said a woman in the front row.

"Was that enough?" asked Nellie.

"No!" a shout rose from several women in the audience.

"No! The powers of darkness have shown their hands once more. Roblin and the Conservatives denied the vote to the women of Carman — when they were legally entitled to it!

"This one small town has been a glowing example of how women can work for justice. The good female property owners of that town planned to throw out their municipal councillors — the ones who were going to hinder the well-being of women and children by approving liquor licences.

"The Hotelkeepers' Association appealed to the government and received help. They complained that Carman was being run by women! Surely this would not be allowed!

"What would *you* do if you were Mr. Roblin? Uphold the cause of women? Ensure their safety and that of their children? No doubt you would. But what did he do instead? He took away their democratic rights! The women went to vote and found their names had been struck from the list — by order in council."

Nellie looked around the auditorium in silence. Some women were nodding their heads in agreement. But some were actually shaking their heads as if they had not heard about the situation before.

"Now, women of the WCTU, what are we going to do about this situation?" Nellie's voice had risen to a well-controlled crescendo. She stood waiting for a response.

A thin wisp of a woman in a light-yellow gingham dress stood up near the front of the hall. "Well, we won't take this sitting down," she said.

Before she could say another word, all the women rose in a spontaneous wave. Jonas Babcock, noticeably, kept to his seat.

The woman in the yellow dress looked around and smiled, but then she said rather feebly, "But I'm just not sure what can be done — with them having the law behind them and all."

"But the law's not fair!" said another, younger voice.

"Well, since when has life been fair?" asked an older woman.

"I've always said that *all* women should have the vote," said Nellie's mother-in-law, "and this incident strengthens my belief. If *all* women had the vote in *all* elections — not just property owners in municipal elections — the government would never have dared to treat us this way."

"This government has taken the law into their own hands," said Mrs. Nash from the platform. "And any government that does that is not to be trusted."

Nellie waited for more comments, but a deep silence followed, so she began, "Let's overthrow this government. We can do it! All we need to do is expose the actions of these men. Manitoba is full of hard-working pioneers who are fair and honest people. They will be outraged if we reveal the truth!"

"Plough a fireguard," a cry went up from the back of the hall. It was Lillian.

"Yes! We'll plough a fireguard against the prairie fire of corruption and oppression!"

A roar of approval went up from the crowd. Then Mrs. McClung raised her hand to speak.

"Yes, tell the province, tell the country! But this will not happen overnight. After all, the news will be travelling by word of mouth. But spread it we must. And while we are at it, we might just as well ask for the vote for *all* women in the province of Manitoba.

"Carman is unusual. It's the only place in Manitoba with enough women property owners to sway the vote, but married women lose their property to their husbands. I repeat, all women should have the right to vote."

"Give women the vote! Votes for all women!" the crowd began to chant.

"I move," said Mrs. McClung, "that we at the WCTU devote ourselves to informing all of Manitoba about the Carman situation and the government's illegal action. I also move that we demand votes for *all* women."

"I second the motion," said Mrs. Nash. "All those not in favour, please sit down!"

Mrs. Nash's gaze swept the audience. Nellie looked over the crowd for signs of doubt. There was a brief moment of tension as someone coughed and shuffled a chair.

But in the end, not a person sat — except Mr. Babcock, who was already sitting down.

"Thank you, ladies, and —" Nellie stopped herself from saying gentleman. Mr. Babcock was already looking red as a beet. He needed no further embarrassment. "Thank you, ladies, you have voted well. And this is just a dry run! You'll have many occasions to vote in the years ahead — and many hotelkeepers to run dry! The last term of office for the governing party was four years, so we can well expect another election in two years. This is a new country and a new century. We can make a gleaming future for our children and our neighbours. Push on, push on to the land where ignorance and greed are things of the past.

"To deny women their rights under law is to deny the principle of democracy. Submission to oppression is rebellion against God!"

Nellie sat down in a rush of elation. They could win the fight and they would!

As she reached over to take the two dozen red roses Mrs. Nash was handing her, she saw Mr. Babcock sneaking out, blowing his nose and shaking his head.

9

Nellie snuggled back into the train seat and glanced lazily at the morning *Telegram*. MOSQUITO MCCLUNG BITES ROBLIN read a headline near the bottom of page three. Not front-page news, but getting close — and in the government paper, too!

Nellie folded the paper over and settled back for a nap. The speech had been a huge success, and now she was heading back home to the family she loved — with a pleasant stopover at Roland to visit Sarah Sayers.

When she awakened, Winnipeg was no longer in view, and a lively conversation was going on across the aisle. A man's voice boomed over the noise of the rails.

"She's a big woman, badly dressed, with a high-pitched voice . . . the rough-and-tumble type. Irish, you know."

Nellie listened more closely. Was he talking about *her*?

"She must have something, all the same," said the woman he was talking to.

"What about her husband?" another passenger asked.

"Quite a decent chap from all I hear. I think more of him since I heard he's getting a divorce. No one blames him either. I guess he got tired of being pointed out as 'Nellie McClung's husband.'"

So the man was spreading false information about her. Well, she would have something to say to *him*!

When the two other passengers went away to freshen up, Nellie swung her chair around — and recognized the man. It was George Peterson, one of Sir Rodmond's workers.

Then Peterson recognized her and all the colour went from his face. "M-M-Mrs. McC-C-Clung?" he stammered.

"The very same!" she answered cheerfully.

"Wh-wh-a-at are you going to *do*? Are you g-going to make f-f-fun of me in one of your sp-speeches?"

"Oh, I'll let you alone. You know it's only the truth that hurts — and your conversation did not show a *trace* of truth."

"I know — but that's politics. You fight to win!" The man had recovered his composure with amazing speed.

"No, Mr. Peterson, you fight *fair*! And that's why I won't drag your name into any speech. You could learn a thing or two about fighting fair and square."

George Peterson looked down at his shoes and his face flushed red.

He spent the rest of the trip looking out the window and trying to avoid Nellie's gaze.

As the train moved into Roland, Nellie rose from her seat, grabbed her valise from the overhead rack, and hurried down the aisle. There were very few passengers left now, and only one man ahead of her was getting off the train. Nellie found herself bumping into the sides of the seats as the train swayed to a stop. When it came to a sudden halt, she lurched sideways and nearly fell into the lap of a woman in the end seat.

"Can't you watch where you're going?" the woman snapped. "Too many businesswomen like you gadding about these days!"

Nellie rushed forward and stepped down onto the wooden platform. The station was nearly empty, and Sarah was nowhere in sight, but Nellie didn't mind. She was grateful for a few moments by herself to hear the meadowlarks singing and gaze at the blue anemones that carpeted the surrounding pastures and headlands. In some places, the fresh earth had been turned by the plough, and in other fields, seeding had begun. Cattle were leaving their winter straw stacks and searching for bits of fresh grass.

"Miss Mooney!" came a voice from the other end of the platform. "I mean Mrs. McClung . . . er, Nellie!"

Sarah appeared, her rich golden hair tied in a knot, no longer in girlish braids.

"I'm so sorry I'm late!" she said, racing over and picking up Nellie's valise. "Mother and I were having a bit of a discussion, and a cow got loose just as I was leaving."

"You *are* busy!"

"Yes . . . and happy. The farm is doing very well."

Nellie felt a surge of pride. Sarah had overcome so much since her father had died.

Sarah led the way to her horse and buggy. "Mother doesn't believe in these new motor cars," she confided, "but I'm not going to wait much longer. It would really save time on the farm."

"Yes, it would be a great help, but do you think you'll always farm?"

"I believe so. I love farming," Sarah answered. "We have a full section now and two hired hands. Of course, I choose the crops and do the running of it. Mother has lost interest."

"How *is* your mother these days?"

"She's quite well, although she's always been delicate. I think it was those bad years back in Wawanesa. She never completely recovered."

In half an hour Nellie and her former pupil had arrived at Sarah's neat, white farmhouse. Nellie went up to the house while Sarah tended to the horse.

"Oh, Nellie, do come into the parlour," said

Mrs. Sayers, greeting her at the door. She seemed to have shrunk to an even smaller size since the Wawanesa days. "I'm so glad you've come. I need you to advise Sarah. I'm terribly worried about her."

Nellie couldn't help wondering what there was to worry about, since Sarah seemed so obviously healthy and happy. The young woman appeared at the parlour door just then, and her face dimpled into a fine smile. "I'll just build up the fire a bit," she said, "and then we can have a cup of tea."

Nellie turned toward the kitchen. "Why don't we all sit in the kitchen and talk?" she suggested. But Mrs. Sayers was shaking her head and motioning Nellie to a wing chair beside the fireplace.

"Sit down, please, Nellie. I must speak to someone about Sarah."

Nellie sat down in the big chair. Mrs. Sayers sat rocking in the small wooden rocking chair beside her.

"You know, Nellie, Sarah will be twenty-four on her next birthday, and she's still unmarried. She'll not have me forever, you know. I'm nearing sixty, and a woman's life is pretty well over by sixty. So marriage is her only safe future."

Mrs. Sayers was pathetic looking, Nellie thought, and her hands fluttered about as she talked. "As you know, Sarah was almost twelve when my husband, Don, died," Mrs. Sayers continued. "The neighbours helped for a few years. Then Sarah took over. It was a good move when we came here to this farm, and she has run it well. But she'll be all alone here when I'm gone."

"The nicest of women do not always marry," said Nellie. "I do believe that men are sometimes blind."

"Well, I wish you'd get Sarah to listen. She is so strong-minded and outspoken. Men do not like strong-minded women, and Sarah says such plain things. She's not one bit ladylike. I don't know what will become of her!" Mrs. Sayers drew out a small lace handkerchief and attempted to hide her face with it as a tear rolled out of the corner of one eye.

"Tea's ready," Sarah called from the kitchen.

Mrs. Sayers jumped up quite nimbly, Nellie observed, and headed into the dining room. Nellie followed.

Sarah was pouring tea into clear china cups. Rose-patterned plates were arranged on the dining-room table, holding hot, puffy biscuits and wild currant jelly. A bouquet of pussywillows graced the middle of the table.

"Mother and I want to ask your advice about something," Sarah said, sipping at her tea. Mrs. Sayers gave Nellie a knowing look as her daughter continued. "We have a problem — or at least Mother thinks it's a problem . . . . Mother thinks I should get married, and I think so too, but I am more careful than my mother and I think ahead."

Nellie grabbed her handkerchief from her handbag and almost choked into it. She could remember poor Mrs. Sayers' drunken and abusive husband. It was certainly no wonder that Sarah was being cautious. But she was surprised by Sarah's direct approach. This was not the timid little girl she had known back in the Northfield School days.

"There's a young man living a mile from here who wants to marry me," Sarah continued. "He's a good fellow, tall with dark brown hair, the right age, and good-looking. In fact, I like him real well."

"So what's the problem?" Nellie asked as directly as Sarah had. Was Sarah being *overly* cautious?

"His father is retiring from the farm now, and his parents are willing to move into Roland, but I will not live in his parent's house," she said firmly. "It's built on the high bank of a creek, beautiful for scenery, but no place for children."

Mrs. Sayers threw Nellie another knowing glance.

Sarah went on. "I told him I was not going to take the chance. He could be careless with his children if he liked, but he couldn't be careless with mine —"

"Has he children?" Nellie asked, slightly bewildered.

"No," said Sarah, unruffled, "but he will have if I marry him, and he's hesitating because I refuse to live in that house."

"Don't you think," Mrs. Sayers said to Nellie, "that all discussions of children should be left until after marriage? It isn't . . . delicate. I was married young, and I knew nothing. I was a very innocent young girl. Girls were innocent then."

"You learned everything the hard way, Mother," Sarah said soothingly. "I look ahead, and, Mrs. — er — Nellie, will tell you I am right. I am not going to get married at all if I cannot settle this. I am not going to fret my heart out with anxiety. I know what those children of mine would do, they'd climb fences — or crawl through — they wouldn't know danger and I couldn't watch them. I'd be busy in the house with a new baby most likely, or one coming."

"Oh, Sarah, what will Nellie think of you! I cannot bear to hear such talk," Mrs. Sayers cried out in real distress.

"Mrs. Sayers, I do not think that you have a thing to worry about," Nellie began. "Sarah has proven to be very responsible. You are living in a fine home. I believe that the farm has been a success, has it not?"

"Oh, yes, Nellie, we've really gone ahead since . . . since my poor Don was taken." Mrs. Sayers' voice trembled a little as she remembered her husband's death.

Nellie too would never forget Mr. Sayers' white face, blotched with purple, as he lay, drunk and frozen, on the Sayers' kitchen floor. Her voice softened as she said, "Since your tragedy, Sarah has never done anything foolish, but has always been there for you."

"Oh, yes, she's been a faithful daughter," Mrs. Sayers continued. "I couldn't have managed without her. She's been a *wonderful* daughter. But now she needs a life of her own."

"And that is why you must let *her* decide," Nellie said in a low, soothing voice. She reached over from her wing chair and put her hand on Mrs. Sayers' trembling arm.

Then, in a louder voice, Nellie added, "And you know, I have a feeling that you're both going to be happy. If this young man cares enough for your daughter, he'll build a *new* house. And I'm sure Sarah wouldn't ask him for the impossible."

Sarah looked up jubilantly as if she were a schoolgirl again.

Suddenly, Nellie was filled with admiration for the young woman. She saw in her a foreshadowing of what women could be — strong, independent, courageous, outspoken, never confusing innocence and ignorance. She hoped that all women would be like this in the future — that they would look out at life and meet its challenges. And where did Sarah get this spirit? Certainly not from her mother, but . . . maybe she had. Children could learn to be opposites. Life sometimes had a way of keeping the balance.

Late the following afternoon, as the train drew into Manitou station, the April sky began to cloud over. Nellie's thoughts were none too sunny either. The train had been held up at Roland for repairs and so was arriving late.

Nellie stepped down lightly onto the cement station platform and looked up as someone came toward her and took her valise. "How was your trip?" asked eleven-year-old Jack.

Nellie stepped forward briskly to keep up to her son, who wasted no time in leading his mother out of the station.

"Where's your father?" Nellie asked. Jack was being unusually brusque. "Has something happened, Jack?" she persisted. "Is someone hurt?"

"Papa's not well, Mother," he said.

"What's the matter?"

"His bronchitis is very bad. He can hardly breathe. I'm sure glad you're home." He turned then and looked at his mother accusingly.

"I hope he's called the doctor," Nellie said.

"No. He wouldn't. In fact, he even went to work until today. And now he's in bed, probably with pneumonia."

"Really? And he wouldn't call the doctor?"

"No, and he told me not to. Said he just needed a day's rest. But I didn't listen. I stopped at the doctor's on my way here. He's probably been up to the house by now."

"He's probably gone by now, too — the train was so late," Nellie frowned. "I hope he left some medicine."

Nellie and her son got into the buggy, and Jack slapped the reins on Jasper's back. Disaster may have been happening at home, but Jack was pleased for the moment. He'd never driven the buggy all by himself before.

"And how are the rest of you?" Nellie asked once they were on the road.

"We're fine. But Alice's mother isn't."

"Oh?"

"Sick too."

"And Alice?"

"Oh, she's gone!"

Nellie looked at Jack in horror. While she'd been away the household had fallen completely apart! "Where did she go?"

"Home. To take care of her mother. She *had* to."

"Who's cooking, then?"

"Florence."

"Florence!" Nellie shook her head. She'd not had much time to teach her ten-year-old daughter the practical art of cooking.

"Yeh, she's not very good. But her best friend, Jessie Wheeler, has been helping."

"And *Horace*?" Nellie asked in increasing dismay. "Who's taking care of *Horace*?"

"Oh, don't worry! Paul's taking care of him. And Alice asked Mrs. Wheeler to check on us as often as she could."

"Well, let's get home! Go as fast as you can!"

Nellie held onto her blue, pheasant-feathered hat as the buggy heaved forward and streaked along the rutted main road.

As she ran into the kitchen, Nellie could smell remnants of mashed potatoes and frying bacon. Florence looked up from washing the dishes and said, "Mama, I'm glad you're home. Papa's awful sick."

Horace ran over to Nellie, leaving Paul behind, pulling a teddy bear in a little wooden cart. "Give Hor-Barrie-Clung a kiss, Mama." The tousled little two year old looked as if he'd been crying. Nellie felt a sharp pang of guilt. She gave him a hug, but she couldn't stay with the children. She had to see Wes. Even as she opened the dining-room door, she could hear her husband's heavy breathing. Nellie hurried through the hall and flew up the stairs.

Gasping and wheezing, Wes was propped up in bed with three pillows behind him. His face was greyish-white and his eyes were sunken. The medicine that Dr. MacCharles had prescribed was on the table next to the bed. But Nellie knew there was really no medicine strong enough to fight pneumonia.

"Wes," she said softly, moving toward the bed and kneeling beside her husband. "Why didn't you send word? I would have come home immediately."

"I'll . . . be . . . ju . . . fine," Wes managed to mumble.

Nellie fought back tears as she lifted his hand to her cheek. The hand was burning hot.

"I'll be right back, Wes," she said in alarm, then raced out of the room and down the stairs.

In the kitchen, she threw on her apron, then hurried into the cellar to dig out some old onions. She filled a pan and brought them up to the kitchen to peel. "Put the tea kettle on to boil, Florence, dear," she said.

She could hear Horace crying in the dining room, but she had to leave him in Paul's hands. She needed to make an onion pack and a mustard plaster as fast as she possibly could.

After she had peeled and chopped the onions, she put them in a pan and placed a lid over them. Then, in a bowl, she mixed equal amounts of dry mustard and flour and added a few tablespoons of baking soda. Next, she poured in half a cup of boiling water and beat the ingredients together. When the mixture was smooth, she rolled it out onto a firm piece of broadcloth and laid the whole thing on a piece of stiff cardboard. Then she took a pot of goose-grease from the side table and headed for the front hall. The goose-grease was in one hand, the bowl of onions in the other. On her way, she nearly collided with Jack. He'd just come in from putting Jasper away.

"Take that mustard plaster, Jack, and bring it upstairs. I'm giving your father a treatment."

"What did the doctor say?" Jack asked, panting his way up the stairs behind Nellie.

"I don't know. Your father wasn't able to tell me. But he left medicine and instructions."

"Mama!" Florence shouted from the kitchen. "It's bronchial pneumonia!" She ran to catch up with Nellie and Jack. "He said the medicine can't help much but it will make him sleep. It's laudanum. And he said he'd be back later this evening."

Fear gripped Nellie's heart as she walked up the stairs with young Jack beside her. "Papa hasn't been well for a long time, has he?" Jack said. Nellie almost gasped at his words, for they were true. Her young son had realized it and she hadn't. She had thought Wes was just worrying too much about the drugstore, but it was much worse than that. How could she have missed the signs?

Wes had been working long hours at the drugstore, and he was always anxious about the prescriptions. He had two assistants, but they were really just apprentices preparing to return to the University of Toronto for their final term in pharmacy. More than once, Wes had caught them making serious mistakes. But they had begged to stay on. So Wes had really been doing the work of three pharmacists, checking everything they did. Something would have to change. Maybe what her mother had been telling her over the years was true. Maybe she wasn't taking proper care of her man.

As Nellie and Jack took their remedies into the sickroom, Nellie could hear Florence coming in behind them. Wes was asleep, but Nellie went ahead and rubbed Wes's throat and chest with goose-grease before laying the mustard plaster over his lungs. The grease would keep the mustard from burning his skin and help the heat from the mustard to penetrate.

Florence sat on a wooden chest next to the west wall, and Jack sat on a small stool beside her. Nellie pulled up a chair beside the bed and checked the plaster from time to time to make sure it wasn't burning her husband's skin.

The smell of onions grew so strong in the room that she shed tears as she watched. Or was she truly crying? She wasn't sure, but when she looked over at her son and daughter, she saw that Jack's eyes were running too and Florence was looking sadly down at the floor.

After she took off the plaster, she and the children tiptoed out of the room. Wes was still asleep. "I don't think his breathing is as laboured," Nellie said.

Jack nodded.

"He sounded a lot worse this afternoon," said Florence.

"Thank you for taking care of him," Nellie said. "You've both been very brave. Now, Florence, would you help Paul put Horace to bed? Then you need to turn in yourself. You've had a hard day."

Florence looked disappointed but headed

downstairs to find her brothers. Jack and Nellie followed close behind.

Just as they stepped into the kitchen, they heard a knock at the front door. Nellie flew to open it.

"Well, I'm back to see that stubborn man of yours," said Dr. MacCharles in his comforting Scottish burr. "He's quite sick, you know." The doctor took off his dripping hat as he stepped inside, and laid it on the chair beside the door. It had begun to rain and Nellie hadn't even noticed. "It's a wet April night out there," said the doctor. "Now, show me where the patient is. I can't imagine him staying in bed."

"He is still in bed, Dr. MacCharles," said Nellie, pointing toward the stairs. A bit of worry lifted as she followed the tall, broad-shouldered man with the greying hair up the stairs to the bedroom. He had helped so many people that Nellie always felt confident when a sick member of her family was in his hands.

Nellie stood quietly while Dr. MacCharles listened to Wes's lungs. Jack came in and stood beside her. Before long, Wes wakened and recognized the doctor. "Sorry to make . . . so much trouble . . . for you, Doc . . ." he said.

"No trouble at all," the doctor said with a laugh. "In fact, you're bringing me business."

"You need . . . business . . . about as much as I do." Wes tried to laugh, but the laugh caught in his throat, and he began choking on a dry cough. Nellie feared the pneumonia was tightening.

"I think it's slightly better than it was earlier this

evening," said the doctor. "Here's some cough syrup that should help." Dr. MacCharles whipped a large white handkerchief from his vest pocket and turned to Nellie as he wiped his eyes. "Those onions, they are strong, aren't they?"

"One of my mother's remedies," Nellie said. "They should work."

"If they don't . . . kill me first," Wes gasped.

Nellie began to laugh but then felt like crying, so she stayed silent.

"I'll be back in the morning," said Dr. MacCharles. "Get some rest now."

As they were going down the stairs, Dr. MacCharles told Nellie the whole story. "He doesn't need water drawn from his lungs now, but he may yet. If there's any change in the night, don't hesitate to call on me."

"I will," Nellie said and let him out the front door.

Nellie stood at the door for a few minutes, with her hand still on the doorknob. Illness and misery come to everyone, she knew. Even her hardy mother was not doing well these days. But Wes — surely not Wes. He was too young to be ill like this. And if he died, she would be a widow at the age of thirty-five, with four children to take care of all on her own.

Nellie shook off her black thoughts and turned back toward the stairs. There, right in front of her, was young Jack. He was sitting on the bottom step with his head in both hands. Poor child! Nellie thought, gazing at him. He was almost sick with worry.

"Jack, aren't you feeling well?" Nellie said, taking off her apron and sitting down beside him.

"Will Papa die?" he asked.

Nellie put her arm around him. "No, Papa will not die. There is no danger of that," she said. "Your Papa is young and strong, and bronchial pneumonia is not as serious as the other kind." She didn't quite believe her own words, but it felt good to say them.

"But could it kill him? Did it ever kill anyone?"

Nellie looked at Jack's serious, young face. She could not lie to him. She knew that bronchial pneumonia could kill. So she answered simply, "Yes, but . . . "

"Well, then," he cried, "tell me this. If Papa died, would you get married again, ever?"

Nellie looked down at Jack in shock. What on earth had brought on this added worry?

"You surely wouldn't," he said. "I'm not as worried about myself as I am for Paul and Horace. You know what stepfathers are like!"

Then Nellie knew what was on his mind. "There will be no Murdstones in our family," she promised solemnly. Jack had been thinking about the story of David Copperfield that she'd been reading to her children lately. "And I would have no reason to marry if your father died. For one thing, I love your father so much I would not want to marry anyone else. For another, I would not need to marry for money. Your father has enough insurance to take care of each one of you. Besides that, we own the house and the drugstore, and I could earn money teaching school. School boards do hire married women who are widowed. So we would manage."

She looked sideways at her son, who still looked worried. "And besides all that, your father is not going to die. He'll be much better in the morning. You'll see." Nellie tried to sound as cheerful as possible, and it seemed that Jack believed her, for the tension left his face. He looked more like a little boy again as he sighed and stood up.

Together they walked out to the kitchen where Paul and Horace were sitting at the table, eating lemon cookies with fresh, warm milk from the neighbour's cow.

"Look, Mama," said Paul. "We're having a party!"

"Yes, dear, I see," said Nellie. She smiled at her daughter who had brought the cookies up from the cellar crock and was now wiping up the crumbs. "What a good idea, Florence!"

Her daughter's eyes brightened and a smile lit up her face.

Soon the children finished eating, and Nellie said, "Now go up to bed, everyone. I'll take care of Horace."

Later that evening, Nellie applied another mustard plaster. Then, as night fell, she sat beside the bed, looking tenderly at her husband and putting cool washcloths on his burning forehead. She watched and prayed till after midnight.

By morning the fever had broken, and by the time Dr. MacCharles arrived, Wes was much better. Nellie breathed a deep prayer of thanks to God. But she knew Wes would become ill again if something did not change.

Nellie and Wes were sitting on the back stoop, watching Horace and Paul play outside their new tent. It was one of those green and golden days in late June. The wheat was high enough to ripple in the wind, like an ocean on a calm day. Nellie took Wes's hand and squeezed it tight.

"Do you think it's really a help to sleep out in the tent?" Nellie asked. Dr. MacCharles had recommended it as a way of restoring Wes's health.

"I don't know, Nellie. I don't know."

Nellie looked sadly at her husband. He had recovered from the pneumonia, but he was still as thin as a rail. And he was working long hours at the store again. Life was turning into a vicious circle. If things went on like this, Nellie knew she might lose him, and she felt that she couldn't bear that.

"Would it help if I stopped my speaking and reading engagements?" Nellie asked.

"No, Nellie. I'm as upset as you are about the condition of women in this province — and you'd be letting so many people down."

"I know that, Wes. But I'd do it if it would make you better."

"No, Nellie, you have to keep going now," Wes said, taking Nellie's hands in his. "This Carman scandal is really a blessing in disguise. If you keep telling people about it, they'll realize how misguided Roblin is."

"He *did* play into our hands. He doesn't realize it yet, but he will!"

"There'll be another election in two years, and that gives you enough time to get the word out about the party politics the Conservatives are playing. Women in Carman need their voting rights reinstated, and we'll need a new government to give them a second chance to vote."

"A second chance . . . . I like that. I think you've given me the title for my next novel! *The Second Chance*. But we have a problem on our hands right here, Wes. There's no point in pulling *women* out of misery if *you're* miserable!"

"I'm not miserable! Life has its ups and downs. We have to accept them."

"But I've been thinking, Wes. You're not gaining back your strength. Why don't you give up being a pharmacist?"

Wes looked up at her, his deep blue eyes showing relief. "I didn't want to suggest it, Nellie, for then all my training would be wasted."

"It wouldn't be wasted. You'll always know about medicines. But the work doesn't suit a temperament like yours. You're so conscientious. We should put the drugstore up for sale."

"But what would I do?"

"We could buy a farm and rent it out. That income and the interest from my royalties would keep us very well in this house, the one that you have already paid for with your hard work. Wes, you've earned a rest."

Wes was about to give Nellie a big hug when they were interrupted by the sound of someone running through the kitchen. It was Jack. He slammed the screen door, pelted out of the house, and ran into the backyard. "I've written a poem for you!" he exclaimed, coming to a standstill in front of them.

"What an honour!" said Nellie. "Will you recite it for us?"

"Of course I will. Here it is —

Good old Wes
Would worry less
If he were free
From the store's distress."

Wes smiled at his oldest son. "I think you've hit on something, Jack."

10

Nellie sat huddled in misery across the desk from Dr. MacCharles. Her tweed skirt and yellow jersey peeked through the front of her old red wool coat. "If this were a man's disease, they would have found a cure long ago."

Dr. MacCharles sat back in his chair and tapped his pencil against the volume of Burns' poetry lying on his desk. Then he looked up, but before he could say one word, Nellie was talking again.

"Something should be done, doctor. Women have endured too much for too long and said nothing."

Dr. MacCharles' keen but kindly eyes rested on Nellie. "But Nellie, you've gone through this with all four of your previous pregnancies. Why are you so upset now?"

"Well, Wes is starting a new job as an insurance salesman in Winnipeg next month. So we were all set to move. And now . . ."

It was early March of 1911, and Wes had been offered a job, to start immediately, with the Manufacturers' Life Insurance Company.

"I'm sure you'll manage fine — just as you always have."

"You know, doctor, it isn't that I don't want another child. It's just that this sickness is so unnecessary. I want to move on with my work."

"More writing? Or is it the readings?"

"It's both. But the most important thing is my work for women."

"I hear that *The Second Chance* was a great success. You must be pleased."

"I was until this nausea hit me. Now, I can't do public readings or anything but try to survive each day."

"Why do you worry about doing readings? I heard the book sold out in one day!"

"Yes, it did. But after my readings, I usually give a speech about votes for women. And now I can't. This infernal nausea is such a waste. I know you couldn't help before, but I thought a remedy might have been found by now." Nellie raged inwardly on behalf of all women as she leaned toward the edge of the doctor's desk.

"But you know what people say — 'Women must suffer; it keeps them humble!' Something would have been done if this were a man's disease." Nellie was not thinking about herself then, but about all the silent, overburdened women of the world — Mrs. Sayers, Mrs. Wheeler, and little Jennie Gills. The walls in the doctor's office blurred. Tears filled Nellie's eyes.

But she wiped her eyes before the tears could stream down her face, and blew her nose. Tears were not the remedy. Women had cried too much already. She sat back in her chair, staring at the doctor.

Silence hung heavy in the room.

Then Dr. MacCharles began speaking in his comforting Scottish burr. "I agree with you, Nellie. Women do bear the burden of childbearing. No one could say that's fair. But then many things in life are not fair. As you already know so well, human justice is something we must work for. And remember, though most women are not as physically strong as most men, they are stronger to endure. Women are better patients than men, and all doctors know it."

"But when will medical science offer some relief?"

"Medical science is only in its infancy, but great strides will be made in the next few decades. By the time Florence is a young lady, a remedy may have been found. And if not in her lifetime, perhaps in her daughter's. But we must work for it, Nellie."

"I'll do my best, doctor," Nellie said as she buttoned up her coat. "Thank you for your time. I'm feeling a little better already."

Nellie stepped out into the raw wind and headed south along Main Street. The little town looked drab and tired on this cloudy day, but she knew she'd miss it. By the time this baby was due, in

October, they'd be living in Winnipeg, and some unfamiliar doctor and midwife would deliver it.

Nellie pushed on to the post office, feeling the benefit of the fresh air. Mrs. Brown waved at her from across the street. She was doing errands again, but she had help this time — from a new farmer who'd begun courting her after buying a section across from her acreage. Nellie envied her. She'd had all her children and wouldn't have to go through this sickness ever again.

The Reverend Mr. Young lifted his hat and smiled proudly at her as they passed each other on the board sidewalk. Young had gone so far as to mention women's rights in one of his sermons the month before. "'There is neither Jew nor Greek, slave nor free, male nor female,'" he'd quoted from the Book of Galatians, "'for you are all one in Christ Jesus.'" Nellie would never forget that day. He'd caused quite a stir.

With Wes in Winnipeg on business, and all the children now in school, Nellie had a bit more time to work on her writing. But she often felt so ill she could barely do anything at all.

By noon, Nellie had finished her errands and was in a much happier mood. At the post office, she'd picked up a letter from Mrs. Nash. And she was also beginning to feel less nauseous. As she turned into the lane leading to her house, she was even considering a meal of bacon and eggs.

Here's more grist for your mill, wrote Mrs. Nash. *Do*

you remember Mr. Babcock? He was the Conservative member Lillian brought to the WCTU meeting you spoke at back in 1909. That was when we first started exposing the Carman affair.

Nellie remembered him well. He'd seemed so out of place among all the women.

Well, Mrs. Nash continued, Lillian was interviewing him for a piece in the paper the other day, and he made a confession. He's defected to our cause! These are his very words: "Women are human," he said. "They have a right to their own voice." And then admitted that we have a right to vote, simply because we're citizens! He said exactly what we've been saying all along. It's a radical move — it means political suicide for him in the Conservative Party. He'll have to go over to the Liberals.

The election has been called for June 11, and it will be fun to watch. The Liberals may not win, but the Conservatives will likely get fewer seats. And that should help our cause.

Nellie knew that many Liberals did not approve of votes for women. But the party was generally supportive.

She read on.

Lillian had an interview with the premier recently and picked up a few words of wisdom from Roblin — about votes for women. "This will wear off," he said. "Women are weaker than men — God made them so." We read that quote at our women's group — the Local Council of Women — and had a good laugh about it!

We're thinking of making it the topic for debate at the next meeting.

Meanwhile, conditions for female factory workers are as bad as ever. One of our WCTU groups is offering English training to young immigrant workers in the North End, and two of the students died recently, within weeks of each other — one of consumption and the other of pneumonia. Those women are weaker than men like Roblin — but it's through no fault of their own. I've a mind to kidnap him and take him down to those factories for a day — and see what he has to say then!

Nellie put the letter on top of a cupboard and went carefully down the stairs to the cellar to get some bacon and eggs. Back upstairs, she laid five wide strips of bacon in the frying pan, humming as she worked. With women like Mrs. Nash and Lillian Thomas in the battle, it would not matter if she was lain low for a few months by a bit of morning sickness. She'd soon be on the speaking circuit again. And by this fall, she'd be in Winnipeg, right in the thick of the political action.

Just then, she heard a thump on the front porch. She rushed toward the door, opened it, and saw before her startled eyes a crumpled figure sprawled out on the porch floor. It was Abe Smith. He must have wandered in and sat down in the wicker chair in the corner and then fallen over. His torn coat had flipped over his head, and the chair had landed on top of him. Nellie bent over and pulled the chair away.

It was not uncommon for Abe to arrive at the McClungs' in this state, but usually he was accompanied by the local policeman. Nellie had asked the officer to bring Abe to her home whenever he fell into one of his drunken stupors. She would then take care of him until he had recovered enough to manage on his own. After each episode, Abe thanked Nellie profusely and solemnly vowed never to drink again. But although it did not happen frequently, Abe always did relapse. And here he sat now. Had he found his way alone today or had the policeman left him in the cold porch?

Abe was in terrible shape. It wasn't only the liquor; the chilling cold had penetrated his old woollen coat and he was shaking as he lay there in a heap.

Nellie tapped Abe on the shoulder. He looked at her through bleary, wandering eyes. She wasn't even certain that he recognized her. "You'd best come inside," she coaxed.

He didn't move. "You'll freeze out here," Nellie said a little sharply. She pulled the storm door open, then pushed the inside door back and waited. Slowly, Abe rose and stumbled into the front hall. He fell against the wall but managed to regain his balance. Nellie followed him inside and shut the door. By that time, Abe had found a seat on the bottom step.

"Now let's go out to the kitchen. I'll make you a nice cup of coffee. That'll warm you up," Nellie promised in a soothing voice.

She walked over to the kitchen sink and filled the coffeepot with cold water and coffee grains. Then she set the frying pan on the front of the stove beside the percolator. Maybe she could convince Abe to eat some bacon and eggs too.

As the bacon curled into crisp, brown pieces, Nellie picked up a pitcher of milk from the cupboard and set it on the table. Then she cracked the eggs she'd put aside and dropped them into the pan beside the sizzling bacon.

She went back to get Abe. He was still sitting on the stair and was shaking with chills. "You must come out to the kitchen," she said. "I've made some coffee for you."

He rose slowly but staggered so much he looked as if he would fall any minute. She put her arm around his shoulders to steady him. They did manage to make it to the kitchen, where Abe sank down onto the kitchen couch.

Nellie hurried over to the table and poured a cup of coffee, adding several spoonfuls of sugar and a little milk. The man had probably not eaten at all today, either. A fresh wave of sympathy went out to poor Abe, who was so enslaved to his habit. With it came a wave of resentment toward those who sold him the liquor.

Abe held the cup in both hands and took small gulps. Nellie sat on the rocking chair beside the couch, watching, in case he dropped the cup. She did not want him to burn himself. Finally, when he'd finished, she smiled at him and said, "Now let's eat. The bacon and eggs are ready."

He nodded as though he understood, but then he sprawled out on the couch, and immediately his eyes closed. Nellie unlaced his heavy boots and pulled them off. Then she took the patchwork quilt from the foot of the couch and covered him.

Already he was breathing deeply. He would not waken for hours.

Nellie scooped the whole panful of bacon and eggs onto one of her blue-willow dinner plates. She dropped two pieces of bread into the frying pan, still sizzling with bacon fat. Then she took them out and set them beside the bacon and eggs.

As she sat eating, she felt badly about the poor drunken man asleep on her couch, but it did not spoil her appetite. She was surprised at how good everything tasted. The nausea must be over, she thought with relief.

Instead of coffee to finish her meal, she poured a full glass of milk from the pitcher. It had been taken fresh from a farmer's bucket that very morning. She took deep drafts of the warm, foaming liquid and sighed with satisfaction.

It was a bright June day, and the air was full of the scent of pea vines and wolf willow blossoms. At high noon, the train pulled out of Manitou station, bound for Winnipeg, carrying Nellie, Wes, and all the children but Jack. He was staying behind for a week to write exams.

Nellie smiled at Wes. She was looking forward to being in Winnipeg as much as he was. She already knew people in the big city — Mrs. Nash and Lillian Thomas — and Winnipeg was the hub of political activity in Manitoba. She was needed there more than ever now, since the Conservatives under Sir Rodmond Roblin had just won the election on June 11. It all made perfect sense. Nellie settled back in her seat for a little nap.

"Mother," came a voice from across the aisle.

Nellie turned to look at Florence. Her only daughter was twelve now — and since her birthday in January, she'd stopped calling Nellie "Mama."

"What is it, Florence?" Nellie asked.

"I wish we could've stayed in Manitou."

"Well, we really didn't have much choice," said Nellie, looking in surprise at her daughter's solemn face. She had thought all the children were happy with the new adventure.

"I know we have to go because of Father's new job, but I still don't like it. In fact, I just hate leaving all my friends behind."

"You'll make new friends, dear."

"No, I won't . . . at least not as great a friend as Jessie Wheeler. And what about Alice?"

"Well, Jessie can come to visit — and you know that Alice will be coming to live with us in Winnipeg after harvest time.

"I know, but it won't be the same. In September, I'll have to start at a new school just to finish my Senior Fourth. Jack's already in high school so it doesn't matter. He's with a new class every year anyway. And Paul and Horace can go to public school together. But I have no one. It's just not fair being the only girl!" Nellie looked over at Paul and Horace, sitting together. She could understand how Florence felt. Paul was pointing at something out the window, and Horace was laughing loudly.

"Well, maybe this next baby will be a girl. Then you won't be so outnumbered."

"I hope so," Florence said with a sigh.

11

"The WCTU are having a few problems in Brandon," Mrs. Nash shouted over the noise of her Oldsmobile. She and Nellie were speeding along the main highway between Winnipeg and Brandon at twenty miles an hour — three times faster than a horse and buggy could travel. Unlike many cars, Mrs. Nash's had a canvas roof and clear cellophane side flaps. There wasn't a cloud in the sky, but it was nice to know they wouldn't be rained on in any case. It was also a relief to get out into the open prairie once more. There was room there to breathe.

Winnipeg was not far from Manitou, but it was a different world. Streetcars wove the city together like shuttles, with their flashing blue and green lights, and their clanging bells. Nellie loved the crowds that surged along the streets at night, and the good times they were having. The children had found new friends, and baby Mark had been born in October. But there were times when she was homesick for the prairies, so it was good to be near them again — especially in May when the trees were coming out in bud and the meadowlarks were settling in for the summer.

"What kinds of problems are they having in Brandon?" Nellie asked, trying to stay balanced in the seat as Mrs. Nash swerved to miss a horse and buggy. Claudia was driving Nellie out to Brandon to give readings from *The Second Chance* at the Town Hall, followed by a speech about the work of the WCTU.

"It seems the women want to put in a playground on the school property there, but the school board won't allow it."

"Why not? You'd think they'd be in favour."

"You'd think so, wouldn't you! But it seems they feel they'd have to pay for more supervision. Some even complained that the children might break windows if they played ball on the premises."

"Quite a number of the board members must be fathers," Nellie said. "I'm surprised they're not more considerate."

"Money talks, sad to say," said Mrs. Nash.

"One day, school boards and educators will put the education and welfare of our children ahead of their pocketbooks," Nellie said. "That'll happen when women sit on the boards."

"I hope you're right. And now, Nellie, I have another request. I would like you to help me do something about women's working conditions in the North End of Winnipeg."

"I'll do whatever I can."

"I'm glad to know you're with me on this. I've told you what things are like there. But there are new problems. Outbreaks of typhoid fever and smallpox have been starting up and spreading like an epidemic. The death rate of babies is still very high, and the survival rate for small children is not much better. And the factories are getting worse all the time. I've brought the issue up at several meetings of the Local Council of Women, but no one has thought of a plan of action. That means I need to go ahead and do something radical myself. So I'm going to visit the slums and factories of the North End on my own initiative. And I was hoping you could come with me."

"I'd be glad to make the trip," said Nellie, "but why does it seem radical to go to the North End?"

"Well, I want Sir Rodmond to go with us."

"The premier! How on earth would we get him to come?"

"Lillian and Frances still have connections with his office. Do you remember the interview Lillian had with the premier last March?"

"How could I forget?"

"Well, I think I can get us an interview, too. Then we'll see what we can do."

"It would be a great privilege to be part of this!"

"And I would be honoured to have you come with me. I have great faith in your persuasive powers, Nellie. I think we'll be able to convince him to come with us on a trip to the North End and the factories."

"Then we'll persuade him to make changes!" Nellie said.

Mrs. Nash looked sideways at her. "Right you are. One step at a time, and we'll change everything!" They smiled at each other in agreement.

Four hours later they were in Brandon, driving up a wide street and watching for the Town Hall. Soon they came to the well-lit building. As they passed it, they saw that the parking area was crowded. There were already a number of buggies inside the adjoining sheds, and quite a few cars parked on nearby streets. So they went a block beyond, and there Mrs. Nash brought her car to a stop at the side of the street.

"We're here," said Mrs. Nash. "Are you ready?"

"As ready as I'll ever be," Nellie smiled. She picked up her bag of books and walked back to the Town Hall with Mrs. Nash.

The hall was a spacious building, and the seats were almost filled. But Nellie felt less nervous after the president of the Brandon WCTU invited her to sit beside her on the stage. Nellie followed quietly, secretly glad that she'd bought a new, soft green velvet dress with a high, white-lace collar and white-lace cuffs. It was her first new dress since her last pregnancy, and it was the latest style.

After a brief introduction, Nellie stood at the podium and said, "I am going to read from my novel *The Second Chance* — a part of the minister's message at the funeral service for a man who died in an accident caused by his own drunkenness. This man leaves behind a grieving wife and daughter." Nellie did not add that this man in her story was, in fact, based on a real person, Don Sayers, Sarah's father. She began.

"'Here is a man who is a victim of our laws,' the minister said, in beginning. 'This is not an exceptional case. Men are ruthlessly murdered every day from the same cause; this is not the only home that it has darkened. It is going on all over this land and all the time because we are willing, for the sake of a few dollars' revenue, to allow one man to grow rich on the failings of others. We know the consequences of this; we know that men will be killed, body and soul, that women will go broken-hearted, that little children will be cheated of their childhood. This scene today — the dead man in the coffin, the sad-faced wife and child, the open grave on the hillside — is part of the Traffic. They belong to the business just as much as the sparkling decanters and the sign above the door.'"

Out of the corner of her eye, Nellie could see an infuriated little man in a dark brown suit snapping the case of his watch and squirming in his seat. She did not allow his impatience to divert her attention, but she knew a storm was brewing.

Nellie continued, reading the last paragraph she had chosen for the event:

"'Everyone of you, no doubt, has foretold this day. I wonder, have you done anything to prevent it? Let none of us presume to judge the brother who has gone. I would rather take my chances before the judgement seat of God with him, the victim, who has paid for his folly with his life, than with any one of you who have made this thing possible. 'Ye who are strong ought to bear the infirmity of the weak.' I do not know how it will be with this man when he comes to give an account of himself to God, but I do know that God is a loving, tender Father, who deals justly and loves mercy, and in that thought today we rest and hope. Let us pray.'"

Tears glistened in the eyes of many in the audience. Then the quiet clapping rose to thundering applause as Nellie shut her book and sat down. When the applause had diminished, Nellie stood again and said, "Now, ladies and gentlemen, I want to invite you to stay for a discussion of the work of the WCTU and perhaps even some political matters. I will speak only briefly. In fact, I'll give you plenty of time to ask questions. But first, I must phone home." Nellie left the podium and walked swiftly into an inner office, while the women of the Brandon WCTU headed for the refreshment table.

The phone rang only twice before Wes's voice came on the line. "Well, how are things at the homestead, Wes?" Nellie asked.

"Everything is fine," Wes said cheerfully. "Jack and Florence are doing their homework on the dining-room table. Paul and Horace are in bed, and I'm settling down to read the newspaper."

"And how's Baby Mark? Did he take his feedings all right?"

"Just fine, Nell. Florence was a great help. She's

finally forgiven him for being a boy. And you know I'm an experienced father by now. A six month old can't get the better of me. He's sound asleep."

"And how are *you*, Wes?" Nellie sounded a little anxious, but she knew she didn't need to be. Wes had recovered completely since he'd left the drug-store and they'd moved to Winnipeg. He was enjoying his new job and the lacrosse league at Manufacturers' Life.

"Couldn't be better."

"I must go, then," Nellie said.

"You tell 'em, Nell. I know you can, and I'm here rootin' for you."

"Thanks, Wes. I'll see you tomorrow. We'll leave early and should be back around noon."

"Goodbye, dear. I love you."

Nellie walked back to the stage with a smile on her face. Wes's support of her work always helped. As she stood at the podium again, she'd even for-gotten about the nasty little man who was still glar-ing at her from the front row. He was red-faced and seemed ready to burst. So Nellie decided to reverse the order of her presentation.

"I wonder if there are some questions before I speak further. Perhaps we could deal with those first."

The man was on his feet in an instant. "I'm going to point out to this fine audience that we should have no respect for any mother who deserts her children." He spoke in a pompous manner with a loud, clear voice, as if he were accustomed to audiences. "For should Mrs. McClung not be at home with her children at this very moment?" He turned to Nellie. "Correct me if I am wrong, Mrs. McClung, but do you not have a six-month-old baby?" Before Nellie could answer, the little man turned to address the entire crowd. "Mrs. McClung would be better employed at home, taking care of her children, for after all, that is a woman's highest duty." Still standing, he swivelled around in a semicircular motion and surveyed his spectators.

Nellie walked to the edge of the platform and paused long enough to get the strained attention of the audience. She looked down at the man in a kindly way and said, "First of all, you can settle down and not worry about *my* children. I have just phoned home to check. They are well and happy, clothed and fed. The baby is in bed, and all is well. Secondly, you're quite right in saying that our children are our greatest assets. You and I are in agreement there, and while it is true that you cannot do anything for *my* children, there is something you can do for the children of this community. Help the women who are trying to make the school board see that a safe playground is needed.

"I hear that some tight-fisted, short-sighted, mean-souled members of the school board are holding out against it, saying it's a waste of money. Of course, I know such sentiments are foreign to you — for you evidently are a lover of children, even taking thought for mine!"

The audience broke loose with laughter and applause. "He's the chairman of the school board," a woman's voice shouted out from the left side of the hall. Nellie pretended to look at her notes, though she had none. She did not want the chairman to see her stifling a smile.

Then Nellie began again. "Children are not a handicap in the race of life. They are an inspiration. We hear too much about the burden of motherhood and too little of its benefits. The average child does well for his parents and teaches them many things. A child pays well for his board and keep.

"But what do we mean by motherhood? Some would say that women are the only ones responsible for the education of their children. And if anything goes wrong, they are blamed. But how can mothers be blamed when the communities they live in refuse to help their children become good citizens? How can women take full responsibility if school boards refuse to provide good facilities?"

The chairman of the school board puffed out his cheeks and coughed.

"It is for this reason that women like us at the WCTU have become involved in public affairs. We are working against corruption, so our children and all of society can benefit from moral mothering."

A woman wearing a large corsage shifted in her seat and looked down at her feet. The flowers reminded Nellie of something, so she added a short unplanned part to her speech.

"Men like Sir Rodmond Roblin would say, 'The hand that rocks the cradle rules the world.' He would say we have enough power already. But if our hands really *did* rule the world, would we have poor playground facilities? Would we have the slums of Winnipeg's North End? No. And I assure you that many of the evils of our world are proof positive that women do not have the power to change things for the better.

"The hand that rocks the cradle rules the world. It's nothing more than a saying meant to keep us quiet. It's a bluff — a bouquet — a cover-up."

At this, the chairman began to look as if he would soon explode. But Nellie did not back down. "Our hands will rule the world," she continued, "only when we have the right to vote. And when we do, the *whole* world will benefit.

"I am a firm believer in women — in their ability to do things and in their influence and power. Women set the standards for the world, and it is for us, the women of Canada, to set the standards high . . . to make Canada truly the land of the second chance!"

The entire audience erupted into applause — with the noticeable exception of the chairman of the school board. As the audience broke up and he rose to leave, he made a special point of coming up to Nellie.

"I *still* think you should be at home darning your husband's socks," he said under his breath.

12

"So nice to meet you, Mrs. McClung," said Sir Rodmond Roblin. "I'm delighted you've come." It was a crisp, wintry day in early December, 1912. Nellie and Mrs. Nash had just been ushered into the premier's office, past the red plush curtains that blocked off his doorway from the outer reception area.

As the months passed, Nellie had kept speaking at WCTU meetings, and going to gatherings of the Local Council of Women with Mrs. Nash and Lillian Thomas. The WCTU supported votes for women, but many members of the council were not willing to fight publicly for justice. So in the early months of 1912, Nellie, Mrs. Nash, Lillian Thomas, and about twelve other radical women founded an offshoot of the council, called the Political Equality League.

The women of the PEL had a broad and daring agenda. They knew there was more to women's suffrage than discussing problems over chicken sandwiches and olives. They had already held one public debate, which Nellie had won by a narrow margin, but the best part of that evening had been the attendance. One thousand people had come — including some of the PEL's opponents, the antisuffragettes. It gave the women of the PEL a good feeling to know that their political enemies each paid half a dollar to see the performance.

And now, Mrs. Nash and Nellie had managed to arrange a meeting with the premier.

Sir Rodmond, a florid, rather good-looking man in his early sixties, walked smoothly from behind his great mahogany desk to greet the two women. He seemed to be in a very genial mood.

"Well, ladies, I'm delighted to meet you, just delighted."

He shook Mrs. Nash's hand and smiled. Mrs. Nash fairly beamed back at him, radiating beauty. Her Persian lamb coat and crimson velvet hat set off her already handsome features to good advantage. The premier seemed favourably impressed.

"And Mrs. McClung," he said, wheeling around on his finely polished shoes. "At last I have the opportunity to meet you — it's a pleasure to welcome you to our great city. I hope you're adapting well."

"We've been here a little over a year now,"

Nellie responded as jovially as possible. "Mrs. Nash assured me that we would like it here, and we do."

"Do sit down, ladies." Sir Rodmond waved them over to a fine leather settee. He waltzed over to his large swivel chair and beamed at them with admiration. He had apparently not expected women suffragettes to be so well dressed and charming.

Mrs. Nash got right down to business. "Sir Rodmond, we have come to ask for a favour."

He answered in a most congenial manner. "And what might two fine young ladies like you have to ask me? I'll do my best to help you."

"We want you to come with us on a tour of some of the factories in your city."

The smile tightened on his face. "The factories?" he stammered. "What on earth *for*?"

"We feel you would like to be informed," Mrs. Nash said boldly.

"Lots of people could inform me — my deputy might be free to go with you. I'll check with my secretary and see if he's free."

"Sir Rodmond, we are looking forward to going with *you*," Nellie said.

"We will not go with your deputy," said Mrs. Nash. "We want to take our premier." She smiled most becomingly.

"Very well," he said, clearing his throat. Nellie took a deep breath and waited, not knowing what to expect. "I will go."

Nellie and Mrs. Nash looked at him with gratitude. Their expressions were not lost on the premier. He smiled at them benevolently as he went directly to the phone on his desk. "Bring my car around," he said into the receiver.

Nellie and Mrs. Nash glanced at each other triumphantly before they stood up and faced Sir Rodmond.

Sir Rodmond put on his brown beaver coat, then said, "This way, ladies," and held the door open. They made their exit in state and headed for a back entrance where Sir Rodmond's limousine was already waiting.

The chauffeur came around and opened the back door. They all piled in, the premier sitting in the middle. Directly in front of him was a cut-glass vase full of real carnations sitting on a small shelf. Nellie could hardly believe what she was seeing.

With his plump hands resting on a gold-headed walking stick, the premier began to speak. "Now, ladies, I will give you my views about these women who work in factories. First of all, I might say, I believe in work. I have always worked very hard. As a boy, I worked from sunrise until the shadows of evening fell — and I enjoyed it. Those were the happiest days of my life, running barefoot under the apple trees."

Nellie and Mrs. Nash listened attentively to his reminiscences. He was obviously enjoying himself. They knew his pleasure would be short-lived after he saw the factories. It was best to let him rattle on. He continued: "Now these factory girls are no doubt idle at home. After all, with the new shortcuts in labour with electricity and such, there is not the work for them to *do* at home.

"But you young ladies are very different. Gentle women, bless them, are often *too* gentle. My, but I love them for it. I can see that you two are this kind and I hope you will never change. These young factory girls, who you think are underpaid, no doubt live at home. They most likely work because they want pin-money. And anyway, working won't hurt them. It will keep them off the streets." He leaned back and tipped his walking stick against the seat.

He really believes he's being fair, Nellie said to herself. Mrs. Nash had told her about his passion for fairness. It made him a very frustrating opponent.

"So my advice to you is this," the premier went on. "Do not let your kind hearts run away with you! And anyway most of the women in factories are from foreign countries, where life was already strenuous. They do not expect to be carried to the skies on flowery beds of ease! It doesn't do women any harm to learn how money comes. Extravagant women are the curse of this age."

Nellie was beginning to feel very frustrated, and her temper was reaching a low boil when Mrs. Nash said in a very calm voice, "There is the factory, Sir Rodmond."

"Stop here, Charles," Sir Rodmond directed, and the car came to a halt directly in front of the building. It had once been a sturdy brick structure with artfully leaded windows, but it was now covered with soot and grime, and half the windows had broken panes. A horrible stench came out of the entranceway as the two activists and the premier alighted from the car.

"It's in the basement, Sir Rodmond," Mrs. Nash

said, bracing herself against the smell and the stiff wind that had just come up. Down the road, Nellie noticed the backyard privies and overflowing gutters Mrs. Nash had described in her letters. A boy in an ill-fitting jacket and light summer shoes was batting a baseball against the loose boards of a weather-beaten fence.

Sir Rodmond, in a show of gallantry, led the way. They all walked cautiously down the dark, slippery outside stairs.

Then they reached a dark hole that exposed a wooden basement door. Sir Rodmond spoke over his shoulder. "Are you sure this is a fit place for you ladies to come? Perhaps I had better go in first." He opened the door and strode inside. Taken aback by the dim light as he walked into the room, he suddenly lurched forward and staggered along the floor, desperately trying to keep his balance. Nellie and Mrs. Nash rushed forward, grabbed his arms, and steadied him.

Once he had managed to regain his equilibrium, the three of them stood still and looked about the airless basement. The great roar of machines was deafening. There was no ventilation and no heat. It was mid-day but the only light came from gaunt lightbulbs, hanging from the smoky ceiling. The floor was littered with apple peelings and discarded clothing.

Untidy women operated the large sewing machines that filled the room. They were bent over, with their eyes rivetted on the material they were pushing under the needles. Their feet were rocking up and down on the treadles in perpetual motion. Equally scruffy-looking men, their backs permanently stooped, were cutting out garments on long tables.

Nellie doubted that any of the workers had heard or seen them enter. She tugged at Sir Rodmond's arm. "Why don't you speak to someone?" She wondered how the workers would respond to a visit from the premier. But Sir Rodmond just shook his head. He could not hear her above the din. His face had gone deadly white, and he seemed to be in a kind of stupor.

"Are you all right, Sir Rodmond?" Nellie asked.

This time he must have seen the concern in her eyes and he nodded, but his face was drawn and there was no sign of the smiling, benevolent man who had led them inside.

After gazing about the room for a few more minutes, he walked over to the nearest woman and shouted, "Does anyone ever sweep the floor in this place?"

The woman looked up for only a brief instant, shook her head, and kept on working.

"These people are paid by the piece," Mrs. Nash reminded him. "They have no time for sweeping." The woman had probably not recognized him, but even if she had, it was doubtful it would have made any difference. Like the others, she would be desperate to keep up with her work.

"Please come this way, sir," Mrs. Nash shouted, directing them with her arm. Nellie and the premier followed.

Nellie thought she heard him say, "Thank goodness," as he turned away from the workers.

Mrs. Nash, however, was not leading him outside, but through a side door that opened into a short, narrow hallway. An even worse smell hit them there. Nevertheless, Nellie closed the door behind her, and when the premier turned around to go back, Nellie gave him a gentle push ahead.

"You can't miss this sight," Nellie said, knowing full well what was ahead, for Mrs. Nash had told her about it.

Sir Rodmond turned and stumbled on for a short distance in the semi-darkness. In a few seconds, they came upon a long line-up of people eating their lunches and waiting to get into a room marked "Toilet."

"They have such a short lunch break that they have to eat here in order to have time to visit the toilet before they return to work," Mrs. Nash explained.

"They have no other toilet breaks. You'll notice," Nellie added, "that there is no separate privy for the women."

"Let's go back," Sir Rodmond's voice boomed out in the hallway. The noise of the machines was diminished here.

"We will, but it's closer this way," Mrs. Nash said, as she led him directly past the toilet. Just then the door opened, and a young girl came rushing out. The stench that came out with her was so rank and sickening that Nellie thought the fresh manure sprinkled on farm fields in the spring smelled like lilacs in comparison.

"For God's sake, let me out of here," Sir Rodmond cried at last. "I'm choking! I never knew such hell-holes existed!"

"These people work from eight to six, Sir Rodmond — six days a week," Mrs. Nash said, hesitating in front of him in the narrow hallway. "But no doubt they get used to it." Her sarcasm seemed to be lost on the premier.

Then, true to her word, Mrs. Nash quickly found an outside door, and Sir Rodmond raced up the steep steps from the basement at twice the speed he had gone down them.

There had been a light snowfall while they were inside, and the limousine was freshly coated in white. The sombre street looked brighter, but the privies still created a stench and the little boy they'd seen on the way in now sat mournfully on an old stump, trying to fish his baseball out of the ooze of the gutter.

Sir Rodmond dove into the car and sat in the far corner, directly behind his driver. He was breathless and sat gasping for a few minutes. The driver waited for instructions.

When she and Nellie were both settled into the back seat, Mrs. Nash spoke out. "Now to the shirt factory. It's across —"

"I know the way," the driver said curtly. "But I'm waiting for the *premier's* orders."

"Now, ladies, I think we have endured enough for one day. I cannot see the point."

"But we would like you to see just one more factory," insisted Nellie.

"I doubt there are any more places like this one," he said. "That has to be the worst!"

"Well, then, you won't mind going to another,

Sir Rodmond. And I must say that the Political Equality League and women of the WCTU are all going to be impressed when they hear of your interest in these poor women. And let me remind you that these women have husbands who are voters."

"Very well," sighed the premier. "I'll go, but I have time for only one more stop. I just remembered an appointment I have right after lunch."

About ten minutes later, the limousine arrived at the shirt factory. It was in a better building and on the main floor, so a bit of light did come in through the windows. But all the work was being done by young girls; a few looked no more than twelve years of age.

"We wanted you to see how these young girls are being kept off the streets," Mrs. Nash said with some sarcasm.

"And what, may I ask, are you people doing here today?" an officious voice cut in, just behind the visitors.

Mrs. Nash and Nellie turned and faced a tall man with a big nose. His beady eyes glared from under bushy, brown eyebrows.

"We have come to visit your factory." Mrs. Nash smiled graciously. Nellie decided the man must be the manager.

"I don't remember giving you an appointment," the man said sarcastically. "So there's the door!"

Sir Rodmond had continued to stare around him with his back to the man. The girls had not raised their eyes when the three strangers and the manager entered. They were obviously also doing piece work.

Now the premier turned slowly and faced the angry manager.

A crimson flush spread over the man's face, and he stammered, "Oh, Sir Rodmond! I'm terribly sorry. I did not recognize you, sir. Do feel free to look about."

"We certainly will," the premier answered coldly.

The manager stepped back as the three advanced farther into the room.

At one machine a girl with wispy, blonde hair worked with an injured hand wrapped in a dirty bandage. "Was your hand hurt on the job?" Nellie asked.

The girl darted a short, quick glance up at Nellie and said, "No, ma'am." Nellie could see the alarm and the pain in her eyes, so she moved away.

At a table across the room, a girl's whole body shook with sharp, piercing coughs while her fingers still flew over the sleeves she was sewing into shirts.

Nellie pointed her out to Sir Rodmond, and together they walked over and stood beside her. She did not look up, but her coughs took on a rattling sound as she attempted to hold them back.

"You have a very bad cold," said Nellie in a kind voice.

The girl looked up then, and *her* eyes were fearful too. "Oh, this isn't a cold. It's nothin' catchin', ma'am. It's just me bronchitis. I gets it every winter."

"Why don't you take a few days off work to recover?" Nellie said. "A little rest might help a lot."

"Oh, no, ma'am. I can't do that. We can't afford it. Me pa, he's out of work just now. And someone has to earn money for food for the family. I was lucky to get this job and me so young." She added in a whisper to Nellie, "Generally, you have to be fifteen to be hired. I'm not quite —" She stopped abruptly and went back to work.

The manager came up behind the girl, looked down and frowned at her. The girl's fingers began to fly even faster.

Then, with a placating look in his eye, he stared at the three visitors and took a large package from under his arm. "I would like you to have a free sample of our fine workmanship here," he said with a smile. He handed his parcel to the premier. "We are indeed honoured, sir, by your visit."

"How often does the factory inspector come by?" Mrs. Nash interjected before Sir Rodmond could answer.

"Factory inspector?" The man looked puzzled. "I've never heard of a factory inspector. In fact," he said, "we hardly need one. All the girls are glad of the work. I have no trouble with them at all."

"How about the girl who coughs so much?" Nellie asked. "Couldn't she be given a few days off with pay to get built up a bit?"

The manager looked at Nellie as if she were a schoolgirl who'd spoken out of turn.

"The company is not a charitable institution," he said, "and makes no provision for anything like that. If the girl is sick, she can always quit!" He threw out his hands expressively in a fine gesture of freedom.

Nellie watched for Sir Rodmond's reaction, but he was moving toward the door and had probably not even heard everything the manager had said. The shirt, still in its package, rested on the table where he'd left it. Mrs. Nash and Nellie followed him.

Back in the car, a subdued and shaken Sir Rodmond stared blankly ahead from his haven in the far corner of the back seat.

Nellie decided to strike while the iron was hot. "Now, Sir Rodmond, do you still think that these women are pleasurably employed in this rich land of wide spaces and great opportunities?"

Sir Rodmond was silent for a minute as though he'd somehow failed to understand the comment. Then he rolled down the window beside him. A cold gust of wind blew away some of the stench they'd brought into the car from the first factory. Sir Rodmond took a deep breath, then said, "I still can't see why two women like you should ferret out such utterly disgusting things."

"Your factory inspector knows about these places," Mrs. Nash said briskly. "Several months ago, we mailed him a list of these conditions. We described them in detail. But he has done nothing."

The premier looked at them sadly. "Why should women interfere in what does not concern them?" he mumbled as though speaking to himself.

"Because we are concerned," Nellie countered, "we have no intention of allowing these deplorable conditions to continue. We would like you to appoint a *woman* factory inspector — a real, trained social worker."

They had reached the Parliament Buildings now, and Sir Rodmond had the chauffeur stop the limousine. He was growing impatient. "I tell you it's no job for a woman. I have too much respect for women to give any of them a job like this . . . but I don't mind admitting that I'm greatly disturbed by all this, greatly disturbed," he repeated. "I'll admit I didn't know that such places existed, and I promise you that I will speak to my inspector about it."

The chauffeur opened the door for the premier, but before he got out, he turned and said, "Now my driver will deliver you ladies wherever you wish."

"That won't be necessary," said Mrs. Nash grandly. "My car is waiting for us." She and Nellie followed him out into the snow-covered parking area. "And we want to thank you, Sir Rodmond. Not all politicians would have come along with us. We are impressed by your caring and your concern."

"Thank you for honouring us with your presence," Nellie added. "I look forward to seeing the reforms you have promised."

Sir Rodmond gave a gracious nod of his head, turned, and stepped inside the Parliament Buildings. Nellie and Mrs. Nash looked at each other and smiled. It was a small victory if not a complete one.

For now, they had done the best they could.

13

It was the middle of December, and the Manitoba winter had settled in to stay. There was a thick layer of snow on the streets, and Winnipegers had taken to wearing fur hats and mufflers.

Inside the McClung's home at 97 Chestnut Street, however, all was warm. In the kitchen, a fire burned in the heater, a canary sang in a cage next to the side table, and a cat lay on the green-and-white-striped couch. Nellie was in an upstairs bedroom, dressed in a pink-and-white-checked gingham house dress, her brown hair done up in a French roll. She was hauling two valises off the top shelf of the closet.

Though Nellie appeared calm and her house was reasonably clean, her mind was in turmoil. It was three-thirty in the afternoon, she had to speak at a WCTU meeting that evening, and she had barely completed her outline. On top of that, Lizzie had just sent a telegram to say that Mother had fallen and broken her leg. Nellie and Wes had plans for nearly every night from now until the New Year, and tomorrow was the only chance they had to go to visit her mother. And as usual, at this late date, just a week and a half before Christmas, she still had most of her Christmas shopping to do.

"There!" she said, thumping the valises down on her bed and trying to remember the opening line of her speech. "Oh, yes, *Women in Manitoba have the legal status of infants!*" But what would she say next? That part of the outline had a gap in it. She opened the middle drawer of the armoire and pulled out two pairs of stockings, then went to the closet and took a starched blouse off its hanger. She grabbed Wes's pinstriped suit at the same time.

"Mother, where are you going?" Paul was in the doorway. He was twelve years old now and starting to have his own opinions about most things.

Nellie threw Wes's suit toward the bed and missed.

"Where are you going? Can I come?" Paul asked, as Nellie bent to pick up the suit. Alice must have forgotten to sweep under the bed last time, she mused as she shook the dust off the pant cuffs. Their household helper had recently enrolled in a deaconess-training course and had begun to cut corners with the housework.

"Your father and I are going to visit Mother,"

Nellie answered Paul. "She broke her leg."

"Wow! I'd like to see that! I'll be ready in five minutes!"

"Hold on, Paul. We're not leaving until tomorrow — but yes, you and Florence can come. I think Jack is even coming. The Christmas exams are over now. But Horace and Mark are staying behind with Alice."

"Hurrah!"

Nellie smiled. "Now, young man, you go and pack."

"Ah, Mother," Paul grimaced, then rushed out to get ready.

Four hours later, Nellie stood at the podium in Grace Methodist Church, where the Winnipeg chapter of the WCTU was meeting. She was going to take a different approach tonight. Instead of focusing on anti-liquor action or women's rights in general, she was going to bring to their attention Manitoba's oppressive laws against women. Despite the factory visit, she was convinced that politicians like Roblin would never pass laws in women's favour.

Not long after the tour with the premier, Nellie had gone to hear two militant British suffragettes speak, Emmeline Pankhurst and Miss Barbara Wiley. They had spoken of the terrible factory conditions in which British women worked — Mrs. Pankhurst had participated in the matchgirls' strikes at two factories a number of years before. Pankhurst and Wiley had also described ancient

British laws still in effect that treated women as if they were property. Nellie was becoming convinced that women were suffering partly because men were passing the laws.

Nellie looked out over the audience. Mrs. McClung was in the fourth row from the front. A group from Carman had come out to give a report on the situation there. Mrs. Claire Graham, one of the Political Equality League's most faithful workers, was doing a last-minute check of the tea table at the back of the hall. Mrs. Nash and Lillian Thomas were sitting on the other side of the room. Lillian was covering the evening for *The Winnipeg Free Press* — and a number of other newspaperwomen were present, since many of them belonged to the WCTU. A few had even decided to join the Political Equality League. Mr. Babcock was not there, but he was on their side now and had, indeed, defected to the Liberal Party. He could often be seen in the noon hour at the corner of Portage and Main, telling the lunchtime crowds all about Manitoba's injustices against women. It warmed Nellie's heart to hear him speak.

The audience stood up for the WCTU pledge, then settled in for Nellie's speech.

"Women in Manitoba have the legal status of infants," Nellie began. "We have no dower rights as do women in Ontario. In fact, we have no rights at all!" She threw up her hands in mock carelessness. "Mothers don't even have a right to their own offspring. A father can put his children up for adoption or assign them to guardians without his wife's consent. He is also allowed to sell the family home or will it away without a thought for his wife's well-being."

The sound of agitated whispering ran through the hall. Some of the women nodded in recognition. Others stared at Nellie in horror.

"The reason these laws still exist today is that nobody knew about them! *But we know about them now!*"

Nellie paused to take a drink of water, then continued. "Perhaps some of you know of other unfair laws."

A red-haired woman near the back of the church spoke out. "I won't give any names, for this involves two neighbours of mine. One of them stole a cow and he was given fourteen years in jail. The other had a daughter who was raped. The rapist was given only five years."

"It makes you wonder which was more valuable in the eyes of the law — the cow or the girl," Nellie responded.

Many women in the audience stared at each other in disbelief and some shook their heads in consternation.

A tall, thin woman stood up in the back row. "It was proven in court," she said, "that a man who lived on a farm near us in Portage-La-Prairie kicked his wife and two children out into a storm. The one child was an infant and died before its mother could reach a neighbour for help. The neighbours all knew about the husband's wild temper. But he was given only *six months* in jail. In the same court at Brandon, a farm hand stole fifteen dollars and a blue silk handkerchief from the owner, and he was sent down for one year with hard labour."

"This is the chivalry of the law toward women, the 'weaker sex,'" Nellie declared. "These laws are a trace of the old barbarism that said women are men's chattels. They belong to the Middle Ages. *Why have these laws not been changed?* Because women have been sweetly ladylike and modest. They have not protested against such injustices, for fear of losing their womanly charm.

"But a great many women are now finding out about these laws and, charm or no charm, they are voicing their indignation.

"These laws are not upheld by all men either. In fact, many men are ashamed of them, but lawmakers are slow to change them. And the women who seek to change the laws do not have the vote."

Nellie caught Mrs. McClung's eye. Her mother-in-law was smiling proudly at her. "Then there are the women who do not *want* to vote. There are three classes of them. The good, intelligent woman who hasn't thought about it, who has a good man between her and the world, and who has never needed to go up against the ragged edge of things. From this class, the suffragists make additions to their ranks every day.

"There is also the young woman who shrinks from being thought strong-minded, the frilly, silly, clinging vine, the girl who wants to be attractive to men, at any cost. This is a form of affectation that many of them outgrow, just as they get over wearing college colours on their sleeves, hanging pennants in their room, and wearing their hair frizzed over their eyes.

"Class C is the selfish woman who does not care, who does not want to be bothered, the cat-like woman who loves ease and comfort, a warm cushion by a cosy fire. This woman will tell you that she can't understand how the militants in England will do such things. In this, she tells the truth, for she cannot understand the unselfish and heroic actions of these English women. Such actions and motives belong to a higher plan of thinking than a cat-woman can ever rise to."

The audience broke out in applause.

"Here is an assortment of caps. Let each anti-suffragist pick her own. Far be it from me to say to which category any woman belongs. I believe 99 percent of women belong to the first and second. I am glad to believe this — their case is hopeful.

"Only fifteen of us here tonight have pledged allegiance to the Political Equality League but I know that many more of you are with us in spirit and that you will be working behind the lines — even though you don't wear the white ribbon. But as our group grows, we hope that more and more of you will bravely stand out with the rest of us, the *suffragettes.*"

Nellie stepped down from the podium as a thundering wave of applause rose to the ceiling.

As she was making her way to the tea table, Nellie noticed a woman in a faded-grey coat, approaching her from the centre aisle in great haste.

"Mrs. McClung, I want to congratulate you. I'm

a visitor from out of town and I am impressed with your speech."

"Thank you very much. This is a very receptive audience."

The woman shook Nellie's hand warmly. "You are a plain talker, and that's a wonderful thing! I will certainly have something to tell our people when I go home. I will tell them I met Nellie McClung, and there sure was no style about her!"

"Well, thank you for coming up to tell me that," said Nellie, trying to take it as a compliment. She knew it was meant that way.

Nellie picked up a cup of tea and took it over to where Mrs. Nash was chatting with a large group of women.

"The press will hear about this meeting and that we are a united force, whether we have all the women on the front lines or not," Mrs. Nash was saying. "With Lillian Thomas reporting for the *Free Press*, we have a sure outlet for good publicity. But the *Telegram* — well, accounts of our efforts have slipped into its pages too, even though it's the government rag!"

"I'm proud of you, Nell," said Mrs. McClung, who'd come up next to Nellie. "I knew you were the woman for this job."

"Well, there's no turning back now — not that I'd want to. I'm in too deep!"

The next morning, before the sun came up, the lights were on in the McClung's kitchen, and Alice was setting bowls of hot oatmeal porridge on the table in front of Horace and Mark.

"I don't see why I can't go!" Horace was pouting. "I'm not a baby anymore. I'm six years old!"

"If you keep on with your pouting, young man, there'll be no puppet show this afternoon!"

Horace sat up straight in his chair and began shovelling the porridge in, a model of perfect behaviour.

"You'll make a fine wife some day, Alice," said Nellie as she entered the kitchen. "You'll find a nice widower and have eight children. I can see it all now."

"Eight! I'd sooner have three, Mrs. McClung. I may be training to be a deaconess, but I'd rather tend that many in church — not at home!"

"You're certainly doing a fine job with our five," said Wes, going over to the stove and pouring himself a cup of coffee.

Fifteen-year-old Jack came striding down the stairs, followed closely by Paul and thirteen-year-old Florence.

"What's on the menu for the morning repast?" asked Florence, who had taken to trying out new words in the most everyday conversations.

"Porridge as usual, Flo-the-slow," said Paul.

"Paul!" said Wes. "Are you coming with us or not?"

"Of course!"

"Well, remember the rules of conversation."

Paul dug into his porridge and stayed quiet until breakfast was over. He continued in silence as the five oldest McClungs finished packing their bags and piled into their new Model T Ford.

But as Wes turned onto the highway leading southwest of Winnipeg, Paul suddenly burst out, "Are you trying to spite someone, Mother?"

"Spite someone? No, Paul. Whatever or who-ever gave you an idea like that?"

"Well, not really someone I know. It was my friend Andrew's mother. He told me at school yes-terday. His mother said that any woman who takes part in public matters must be out to spite some-one — especially if she leaves home to do it!"

"That's so unfair!" said Jack.

"Yes, a miscarriage of justice," said Florence. "Don't listen to such nonsense."

"It's strange, Paul," said Wes, "but when some-one like your mother goes public to change things for the better, many otherwise kind people try to find fault."

"They are resistant to change, even for the relief of their own condition," said Florence.

"You mean they get uncomfortable when some-one sticks their neck out for them?" Paul asked.

"Yes, something like that."

"People are quick to condemn those who break society's laws — even if those laws are rotten to the core!" said Wes.

"Andrew's mother is a kind woman," said Nellie. "She is always the first to take a meal to a sick person or to someone who is poor."

"A Good Samaritan," said Florence.

"Yes, but the Good Samaritan did not just help bandage up the beaten man. He came back to check up on him later."

"And I'm sure," said Wes, "if he'd met other

Good Samaritans on the road, eventually they would have done something to get rid of the thieves who beat the man in the first place."

"That's what I'm trying to do, Paul. I'm trying to get to the root of the problem."

"I'll tell Andrew."

"That's a good idea," said Wes, "but Andrew's mother might never understand. The important thing is to keep standing up for the right thing — even if people criticize you."

Nellie grew colder and colder as they drove along, in spite of the heavy buffalo robe thrown over her knees. The burring sound of the motor was not nearly as soothing as the clip-clop of horses' hooves and the jingling of bells in the harness. But she did not miss the raw wind and the bits of snow thrown up in the passengers' faces from the horses' hooves. Besides, they would not have had time to make the trip by cutter, and a trip by train for five people could not have been organized so quickly.

Nellie turned around and looked at her three oldest children. It was an unusual delight to have them and Wes with her for such a long time.

"Did I tell you about the man at my last speech?" Nellie asked.

"Yes, Mother," said Jack.

"No," said Florence. "I haven't heard it."

"Well, at the end of my speech, he stood up and said smugly, 'Mrs. McClung, don't you wish you'd been a man?' Then before he could sit down, I said, 'Yes, and don't you wish that too?'"

"Mother, how could you?" Florence squealed

above the gales of laughter filling the back seat.

Snow drifted across the road from time to time and the wind set up a howling noise, but inside the black Ford, Nellie and Wes heard nothing but laughter and the occasional back seat spat. Now that she was growing older, Florence, outnumbered though she was, seemed able to hold her own.

It was almost three o'clock by the time they arrived at Lizzie's farm outside Holland. They'd been only four hours on the road, but had stopped at Elm Creek for a light lunch around noon.

Nellie knocked loudly on the front door. The day had darkened, but a candle flickered in the lower window. Like Mother, Lizzie always left a candle in the window as a guide in case someone got lost in a storm.

In a few minutes, Lizzie stood in the doorway, holding a coal-oil lamp in one hand to make sure it really was Nellie and Wes. Then she opened the door.

Lizzie wasted no time in calling her children in for tea and bringing out fresh-baked scones and saskatoon berry jam.

"How's Mother?" Nellie asked, as she set the cups and plates out on the table.

"She's so helpless," Lizzie sighed. "The doctor can't operate because of her age, but he's set the bone in a cast to protect it. She doesn't seem to be in any pain."

"Oh, Lizzie, I'm so sorry. It was always Mother's

worst fear — that she would be a burden on her children. How could God let that happen? She's always been so willing to serve others. And now she has to be waited on. It will kill her!"

"It's not the way you think," Lizzie said patiently. "Mother is content."

"But how can she possibly be content in such a helpless state?"

"You'll see," Lizzie soothed. "You're tired, and you look cold too. Why don't you run in and see her before you start in on tea?"

Nellie walked over to the first-floor bedroom and opened the door cautiously. Mrs. Mooney was dressed and sitting upright in bed, leaning a little against three stiff pillows. She was knitting rapidly, but she hesitated and looked up sharply when Nellie came into the room.

"What kept you, Nellie?" she said. "I would have thought you'd come before now."

"I came as soon as I heard you'd fallen," Nellie said. She went over to the bed and knelt down beside it. Her mother did not appear to be fretting at all. "Are you in pain?" Nellie asked.

"Oh, I have a little pain now and again, but nothing to speak of. What can a body expect at the age of eighty-five? I'm no spring chicken anymore. I must say you're looking well, Nellie. Thank goodness you've finally put on a little weight. What a time I had, getting you to put on an ounce. Your father used to call you Sparrowshins. Do you remember?" Her fingers flew as she started knitting again.

Nellie swallowed as she remembered the father

she'd loved so well. They had been kindred spirits. But she was amazed and relieved to see how content her mother was. On a table in the far corner of the room, two books peaked out from under a pile of *Family Herald* magazines, but they weren't Nellie's. She said nothing but looked down and blinked away a tear.

"Well, I must get this knitting done," Mrs. Mooney said. "When Will comes back for us, we're all going west — John and I and the children. I have to have enough socks and coats knitted. And I've so many rugs to hook. A new log cabin will need warm rugs. I'll never be ready if I don't hurry! And your father's coming in from the barn any minute now."

Nellie stared at her mother in disbelief.

Mrs. Mooney looked right past Nellie as though she were looking out the window. "We'll go in the spring, you know — when this snow has gone. I want to have everything ready. That's why I'm making good use of these days. I don't have any outside work now. So I can get lots of warm clothing ready."

Nellie tiptoed out of the room and left her mother knitting. She burst into the kitchen, where Lizzie and Wes were setting the last places for tea. "Lizzie!" Nellie whispered, "Mother thinks she's back in Ontario. She thinks she's getting ready to go west. And she thinks that Father is out in the barn!"

Unruffled, Lizzie turned and said, "Calm down, Nellie. Mother's not complaining. She loves to watch the pile of knitting she's stacked in her room. And sometimes she's on the homestead again. She tells me how she and Father just went out to look at the crops. She's enjoying reliving those memories. And she's not in any great pain."

Nellie sat down abruptly and realized that as usual, Lizzie, in her quiet way, was right. "If anything changes, you'll tell me, won't you?" she asked, looking up at her older sister.

"Of course," Lizzie said. "Now come and join us for tea."

14

"Sir Rodmond, I'm so surprised! I never dreamt you'd answer your own phone." Nellie was standing in the front hall at Chestnut Street, speaking into the wooden wall phone. She had awakened that sunny April morning, four months after the factory tour, and realized the PEL had still received no helpful response from the premier's office. So she'd decided to cut to the chase and simply ask Sir Rodmond to give Manitoba women the vote.

"Well, I like my constituents to feel I'm easy to reach. I do answer my phone when I'm free. To whom am I speaking and what may I do for you?"

"It's Nellie . . . Nellie McClung. Do you perhaps remember me?"

Nellie heard a stifled cough at the other end of the line, followed by, "Er, yes, of course — I couldn't forget you. In fact," he said, "I've heard a great deal about you, young lady. Most of it very positive. You've become very successful as a writer and speaker."

"Do you remember our visit to the factories last December?" Nellie asked.

"How could I forget that?" Sir Rodmond said with a sigh.

"Would you consider giving me an interview?"

"An interview?"

"Yes."

"Well, I . . . I *will* be free this afternoon at . . ." Nellie could hear pages rustling. "Would you care to come at two o'clock?"

"I'll be there. Thank you, Sir Rodmond." Nellie hung up the receiver quickly before he questioned her further. She could hardly believe her good luck. First of all, who would expect the premier to answer his own phone, and in the second place, who would believe he would give her a private interview at all, let alone so quickly?

Nellie walked across the hall into the study where she now did most of her work. The room had a cosy fireplace set into the east wall, with a settee opposite and a large wing chair on each side. Her small oak desk stood beneath a tall window a few feet from the fireplace. The house was perfectly quiet. Alice had eaten lunch early, put Mark down for his nap, and gone to the market. Jack was living and studying at Wesley College now, and doing very well. Florence, Paul, and

Horace were away at school and no longer came home for noon hour.

So Nellie sat alone, leaning on her desktop with her hand under her chin, looking out the window at the April sky. She was thinking about what she would say to Sir Rodmond. She hadn't really expected to get through to him — at least not so soon.

Nellie had just begun scribbling a few ideas on a notepad when she heard Wes's footsteps in the front hall. He came home from the insurance office for lunch sometimes, and she was relieved that he'd decided to do that today.

"I'm pleased for you, Nellie," Wes said, after he was seated at the kitchen table, chewing on the chicken sandwiches Nellie had just pulled out of their new icebox.

Nellie grimaced. "I don't know. It seemed too easy — getting the appointment, I mean."

"Well, you're always ready for anything, Nell," Wes chuckled, looking directly into her eyes as she sat down opposite him. "You'll do just fine talking to the premier. Think of all the speeches you've been making. It can't be easy talking to such huge audiences — even filling Massey Hall in Toronto."

"At the time, I didn't know it was filled. I couldn't see out into the audience, thank goodness!"

"Well, you weren't at a loss for words then, nor are you when you speak to small schoolhouses full of farmers — where you can see every face in the audience. You always have an answer for everyone. And remember, the premier will at least be polite.

Not like some of the hecklers you've faced down."

Nellie laughed. "Oh, Wes, you know I love having hecklers at my speeches. They sharpen my wits and spice up the evening."

"Most women wouldn't think so," Wes said. "And with all your success, you've not changed a bit. Some women would be putting on airs. But not you! It speaks well of you that you still have birthday parties for all the children — yours and the neighbours' too — and take in people who are down and out. By the way, did you ever hear any more about Abe Smith?"

"We got a letter about him from Reverend Young a couple of days ago actually. Among other things, he said Abe went to live with relatives in Saskatchewan and he's actually sobered up."

"So your help and prayers were not in vain. And he isn't the only one you've helped. Remember that carload, stranded at our cottage on Lake Winnipeg, last summer?"

"Yes. It took them a whole week to fix the car! But, you know, they were interesting young people, and I enjoyed their company."

"It's a good job you didn't tell them who you were until they asked, just when they were leaving. I'll never forget the look of shock on their faces when they realized a famous author had cooked for them all week!"

Nellie smiled.

"Any other startling news from the Reverend?" Wes went on.

"Mrs. Brown got married to that prosperous bachelor farmer who lived across from her farm."

"They're both old enough to retire now, aren't they, Nell?"

"She does have two sons ready to take over. But you know farmers never retire. I'll bet she'll always keep a hand in things."

"Yes, she probably will. Just like you. You're always helping *someone*. You know, Nell, when I come home after a day's work, I ask myself a question. 'Who's coming to dinner tonight? The town drunk or the premier of the province?' Either way, you're always the gracious hostess — you treat all people the same."

Nellie smiled. "I try, Wes. But right now, I don't feel —"

Just then the kitchen door opened. It was Florence.

"Well, young lady, did you forget your lunch?" Wes asked.

"No. It's worse. I forgot my homework assignment." She drew off her high-buttoned boots and ran through the room in her stocking feet. Then she bounded up the stairs two at a time.

"I'll drive her back," Wes said. "Then I'll come back with the car for you."

"Fine, but if you don't make it, I'll just take a taxi."

Florence raced back down the stairs, clutching the coveted scribbler in her right hand.

"Sit down and have your lunch," said Nellie. "Your father will drive you back to school."

Florence sank breathlessly into a chair and leaned on the table as she took a chicken sandwich and a cucumber pickle. A teenager now, she resembled her mother at that age. She was small, with sparkling, brown eyes and bright-brown hair.

"This is great," she laughed. "I should forget my homework all the time! When do I ever have the opportunity to enjoy lunch with both my parents?"

Nellie and Wes exchanged glances.

"Mother," Florence said between bites, "while I have your undivided attention for a few minutes without some stranger here, may I ask you an important question?"

"Of course. What is it?"

"Well, when I turn fifteen, may I have a *big* birthday party? Now I'm in high school, I know more people. And do you know, I've been invited to Janice Little's party next week. She's the most popular girl in our class. I can go, can't I?"

"Yes, I think so. But why are we discussing your fifteenth birthday *now?*" said Nellie. "This is April! Your birthday's not until next January twenty-eighth!"

"But you're so busy, I knew I'd have to get my request in early. You get booked so far ahead."

"Well, yes, I do have a speaking tour the week before that, but I'll arrive home the Friday or Saturday before. That's plenty of time to prepare. So, yes, you may have a party — the best ever yet — one you'll remember forever! And you can invite all your friends from Winnipeg to Manitou, if you like."

Florence still looked skeptical. "And do you *promise* nothing will interfere?"

"I'll try my best, dear," said Nellie with a sigh.

"That's wonderful," Florence smiled. "Now, I'd

better go back. Hurry, Father, I don't want to be late."

Nellie sighed again as she watched Florence and Wes leaving. Her daughter reminded her a lot of herself at that age.

Sir Rodmond's secretary pushed back the red, plush curtain and ushered Nellie into the premier's office.

"Nellie," he said in a most congenial manner as he came around his massive mahogany desk. He shook her hand and added, "Do have a seat."

Nellie, in her light blue silk dress, felt very small as she sat down, as if she were about to disappear into the tall, stiff leather chair the premier had offered her.

Sir Rodmond strode back behind his desk and lowered himself into his swivel chair. "Well, what may I do for you today?" he asked with an amused smile. He took a cigar from the mahogany case in front of him and lit it. He seemed to be enjoying himself.

He thinks I'm an interesting amusement, Nellie thought. Then she spoke out clearly. "Sir Rodmond, I have come to ask you to give the vote to the women of Manitoba."

Sir Rodmond stiffened visibly and the smile left his face. "You know that is a very controversial issue. Do you thrive on conflict?"

"Sir Rodmond," Nellie said, "the women of Manitoba are going to be given the vote, either by you or by someone else, and as you are the present premier, it can be your proud privilege to pass this piece of legislation, and it will then be to your credit."

The premier stared down at his desk. The corners of his mouth were twitching into a bit of a smile.

Nellie continued, "I know what you're thinking. You're not impressed with the importance of this matter, but that's because you never thought of it, and you really should begin to think about it. You can no longer afford to take this attitude of indifference, and that's why I came to see you."

He looked up from his desk and said, "What in the world do women want to vote for? Why do women want to mix in the hurly-burly of politics? My mother was the best woman in the world, and she certainly never wanted to vote! I respect women," he went on, "I honour and reverence women, I lift my hat when I meet a woman. But I see no reason to give them the vote!"

"That's all very nice to hear," Nellie said, "but unfortunately it is not enough. The women of Manitoba believe the time has come for political equality. Our laws are extremely unfair to women."

"I haven't found that to be the case."

"I would like to tell you — and your cabinet — about unfair laws, for I don't believe you know about them, and I would really like to do it this afternoon."

"The cabinet members are all busy in their offices at the present moment."

"It wouldn't take me long. I think fifteen minutes would be enough."

"I don't feel they would be interested."

"If I can convince you and your cabinet that giving women the vote is the right thing to do, it could all happen much more smoothly. It would certainly be easier, more dignified and less disturbing than if we women were compelled to fight for it."

"Fight! You think women will fight for the vote?"

"That is exactly what we are prepared to do — if that is the way you want it!" Nellie said in a low but determined voice.

The premier was now leaning forward over his desk, and the smile had left his face. His mouth was open but no words were coming from it.

In a cheery voice, Nellie said, "I wish you would call your cabinet in, Sir Rodmond. There's plenty of room here in your office."

Sir Rodmond removed the dead cigar from his mouth, and his eyes hardened. "The cabinet wouldn't listen to you."

"You'd be surprised," Nellie answered. "I'm really not hard to listen to, and I don't believe the cabinet would mind at all. In fact," she said brazenly, "I think they'd like it. It would be a welcome change in the middle of a dull day."

Sir Rodmond's face went red as he burst out, "You surprise me. *Who* do you think you are?"

Nellie leaned forward in her chair, and her twinkling, brown eyes became serious now as she said, "Sir Rodmond, at this moment, I'm one of the best advisers that you ever had in all your life. I'm not asking you for a favour, I'm really offering you help."

"What if I tell you that I don't need your help?" he said severely. "And that I think you're a conceited young woman, who has perhaps had some success in Friday afternoon entertainments at country schoolhouses and so you labour under the delusion that you have the gift for oratory. Now what do you say to that?"

"I don't mind," Nellie answered. "I don't even resent it. But I wish to tell you again, Sir Rodmond, as clearly as I can make it, that we, the women of Manitoba, are going to create public sentiment in this province that will work against you at the next election."

Sir Rodmond stared at her coldly across the wide space of his desk. A flicker of doubt seemed to pass across his face. Silence hung heavy between them.

Then Sir Rodmond's mood changed. His self-confidence came back. Nellie thought he was very likely going over his assets. His party was firmly entrenched, and he knew it. He grew jocular.

"It would never do to let you speak to the cabinet," he said as if he were addressing a naughty child. "Even if they listened to you, which I doubt, you would only upset them, and I don't want that to happen. They are good fellows. They do what they are told to do. Every government has to have a head, and I'm the head of this one, and I don't want dissension and arguments. I believe in leaving well enough alone."

"But, Sir Rodmond —" Nellie began.

"No, you can't come in here and make trouble with my boys, just when I have them trotting easy and eating out of my hand. Now, you forget all this nonsense about women voting," he went on in the suavest tone. "You're a fine, smart young woman, I can see that. And take it from me, nice women don't want the vote."

His voice dripped fatness.

"By nice women," Nellie said, "you probably mean selfish women who have no more thought for underpaid, overworked women than a . . . a pussycat in a sunny window has for the starving kitten on the street. Now, in that sense I am *not* a nice woman, for I *do* care. I care about those factory women, working in ill-smelling holes. I *promise* you that we intend to do something about it, and when I say 'we,' I am speaking for a great many women, of whom you will hear more as the days go by."

Nellie stood to leave.

Sir Rodmond smiled good-humoredly at Nellie and said, "Now, don't go away mad. You know you amuse me. Come any time. I'll always be glad to see you."

Nellie's smile was as good-natured as his as she said, "I'll not be back, Sir Rodmond, not in your time. I hadn't much hope of doing any good by coming, but I thought it only fair to give you a chance. I'll not be back, but it's just possible that you will hear from me — not directly, but still you'll hear. And you may not like what you hear, either."

"Is that a threat?" he laughed.

"No," Nellie said. "It's a prophecy." She turned abruptly away, walked between the red, plush curtains, and was out in the hall in no time, heading for the front entrance.

Outside, a fresh April breeze whipped across the parking area as Nellie made her way toward the Model T. A voice called out, "Mrs. McClung," but she did not hear it at first.

"Mrs. McClung," the voice said again. Nellie turned then and looked into the face of T.C. Norris, the Liberal leader of the Opposition.

"Yes?" she said politely, pushing away her thoughts of Sir Rodmond.

Mr. Norris held out his hand to her. "I'm pleased to meet you, Mrs. McClung. I'm Tobias Norris."

"I know," Nellie said, shaking his hand. She had seen him many times when she was in the Visitors' Gallery, watching parliament in session. At this moment, she barely trusted any politician. So she looked at him skeptically.

"I've been wanting to speak with you for a while now," he continued. "Maybe we could talk here for a minute." He hesitated then, as if waiting for her response.

What could she lose by listening? she thought, then asked him, "What would you like to discuss?"

"I understand that you and others are trying to obtain the vote for women," he said calmly. He had a gracious, kind manner and seemed very genuine.

"We most certainly are," Nellie said. She was beginning to like this levelheaded man with the quiet eyes.

"I have a few suggestions then." He hesitated

again, as if waiting for her response. There was no condescension in his manner. It appeared that he sincerely wanted to help.

So Nellie nodded and said cheerfully, "Suggestions are welcome. We can use all the good ones that come our way."

"I feel the time is ripe for you to press your requests," he said. "As you know, next year will be an election year. But we, the Liberal Party, need to know how many people actually do want women to have the vote."

"Our Political Equality League could obtain signed petitions from those who want the vote for women. Would that convince you?"

"Yes. If there were enough signatures, it would convince us. And I'm glad we've had this talk. It was a privilege meeting you. I hope to see more of you."

Nellie smiled and began walking toward her Ford. After she'd taken a few steps, she heard a voice behind her again. She turned.

"Mrs. McClung!" Mr. Norris shouted, with one foot on the running board of his car. "Good luck!"

15

"Well, well, well, it's Calamity Nell!
It's Calamity Nell, can't you tell?"

A knot of young men and women stood chant-ing outside Grace Church the night of January 23, 1914. The words seemed to shatter in the air with their frozen breath. It was a stark midwinter night lightened slightly by an expanse of brilliant stars and a nearly full moon.

Young Conservatives, Nellie chuckled to herself as she rushed up the stone steps. She was slightly behind schedule and had not a moment to lose. The heavy oak doors creaked open and Nellie stepped into the vestibule. Someone was just fin-ishing their organ practice, and the WCTU orga-nizers were rushing around, distributing programmes. Included with them was a pamphlet written by Dr. Mary Crawford, an active member of the Political Equality League. The pamphlet was called "The Legal Status of Women in Manitoba."

Mr. Babcock was directing party workers who were draping banners across the front of the sanctuary. Mrs. Graham was putting three large geranium plants in front of the pulpit. Someone's child was playing with a boxful of "Votes for Women" buttons and had strewn them all over the floor behind the last pew on the right.

Nellie took off her dark blue coat, edged with fox fur, and draped it over her arm. "Oh, there you are, Nell," said Mrs. Nash, who had helped to organize the event. It was being sponsored by the PEL and the WCTU combined and was open to the public.

"It's a big night, Nell, and you're going to wow them. Lillian's covering for the *Free Press* as usual — but we've heard rumours that the *Telegram* is sending someone too. That would be a breakthrough!"

Half an hour later, Nellie was standing in the pulpit of the large sanctuary. She took a deep breath and sailed right in.

"For years, women have been tending the hearth and minding the sick. For years, we have laboured under the delusion that God made women weaker than men — we didn't make them so, God did — so that must mean women had to be subject to men. Some good people of the Church even used their ingenuity and claimed that God ordained the subjection. Like all well-intentioned and misguided people, they forgot one major thing: the part in Galations where it says there is 'neither Jew nor Greek, slave nor free, male nor female, for you are all one in Christ Jesus.'

"Come to think of it, through the ages, people have blamed the Almighty for all sorts of operations they'd botched up themselves. Long ago, people broke every law of sanitation, and when plagues came, they blamed the Almighty and said, 'Thy will be done.' They were submissive when they should have been investigating.

"This is the meaning of the women's movement, and we need not apologize for it. Prevention is the highest form of reform. If we sit passively under unfair and deplorable conditions, we become, in the sight of God, partners with them. Submission to injustice, submission to oppression, is rebellion against God.

"For too long we have believed that it was a woman's duty to sit down and be resigned. Now we know it is her duty to rise up and be indignant.

"So long as women are content to give out blankets and coals and warm woollen mufflers, and provide day nurseries, all is well, but if they dare meddle with causes, they find themselves in politics, that sacred domain, where no women must enter, or she will be defiled.

"Now politics is only public affairs, yours and mine, as well as other people's. You and I are affected by what goes on outside the four walls of our home — the home has expanded now until it has become the whole state. The work has gone out of the home and the women have had to follow it.

"If politics are corrupt, it is all the more reason that a new element should be introduced. Women will, I believe, supply that new element. Men and women were intended to work together. Men alone cannot make just laws for men and women, just as any class of people cannot legislate fairly for another class. To deny women the right of law-making is to deny the principle of democracy."

Some members of the audience eyed Nellie warily, while others nodded their heads in agreement. Others sat in disbelief. For a brief second, Nellie caught Wes's eye from the front pew on her left. His whole face was beaming with approval.

As she made her way through the twists and turns of her argument, she felt, in the back of her mind, that she was giving one of the most important speeches of her life. At times, she lowered her voice to a near-whisper. At other points, she paced across the front of the sanctuary and spoke so loudly she could hear her voice echoing over the crowd. As she completed the speech, she caught Wes's eye again and thought of home.

"The real spirit of the suffrage movement is sympathy and interest in the other woman, and the desire to make the world a more homelike place to live in. Some say, untruthfully, that suffrage for women would destroy the home. On the contrary, it will only destroy the narrowness of the home. It will spread the home spirit until it finds its way into every corner of the world."

Applause broke out and lasted for three whole

minutes. Nellie was thrilled, but she also knew that some people in the audience were not on her side. Even her opponents enjoyed her speeches, though they clapped in appreciation of her dramatic presentation, not what she had to say.

As Nellie turned to go, a commotion in one of the front pews caught her attention. A man sitting just two places over from Wes had jumped to his feet. "Aren't you gonna let us ask questions?"

Nellie had thought she would leave out that part tonight, but nodded and said, "Yes, if you have a question, we would love to hear it."

"Well, it's about that story you told earlier."

"Which one?" Nellie asked.

"The one about the sixty-five-year-old woman who was left nothing when her husband died — only her 'keep' with the youngest son, who inherited everything from the father."

"Yes, I think she deserved more. She had worked as hard as her husband to homestead that farm."

"We must be on our guard against such a sob story," the man said, turning to address the audience. "After all, she was left her keep. She could go on living in her familiar surroundings, happy and willing to help her son's wife and family. Mrs. McClung's big complaint is that she was not left any money. Now tell me, what need has a sixty-five-year-old woman for money?"

He sat down and Nellie let a few seconds pass in silence just to let that last sentence sink in. Then she said, "I thank you, sir, more than I can tell you. You have completed my story better than I could ever have done. What does a woman of sixty-five need money for?"

Nellie looked to a group of elderly women to her right. "Do you ever feel the need of money?" she asked them. "Do you ever want to subscribe to a magazine, or give a donation to a charitable cause, or send presents at Christmas without asking anyone's permission?"

Shouts of "Yes" came from all directions in the audience.

"I am sure you wouldn't want to go to your own son and say, 'Please give me a dollar and a half. I want to buy your sister's baby a present.'"

"No, we wouldn't," shouted more female voices.

Nellie stepped down and went to her seat amid loud, ear-splintering applause.

As the crowd started to break up, Nellie headed over to where Wes was chatting with Mrs. Nash's husband and Lillian's sister, Frances. This was the last night of a two-week speaking tour and Nellie was eager to get home. But on her way toward Wes, she was swept away by a crowd of well-wishers and critics.

"Women do not have the executive ability that men do, Mrs. McClung," said a well-groomed man. Nellie recognized him as one of her neighbours on Chestnut Street. "It would be unfair to women to throw them into public work. They're far too excitable."

"Men are much more stable, aren't they?" Nellie smiled impishly. "Take Henry the Eighth, for example, or Nero! We wouldn't want to suffer anymore under the whimsical rule of a Good Queen Bess."

"But Queen Elizabeth the First was an exception!" cried another detractor.

"Exceptional, yes. And if women had been viewed as equals over the years, there would have been more leaders like her."

"Without the vote, we'll never see another leader like Good Queen Bess, now that we're in a supposed democracy!" said Mr. Babcock, who had just come up to congratulate Nellie.

"Mrs. McClung would make the best leader," said a woman who'd arrived at the end of the discussion. Nellie looked up and was surprised to see Sarah Sayers. She moved away from the crowd to speak to her.

"It's good to see you, Sarah. And who is this?" Nellie exclaimed, noticing a red-cheeked baby in her arms. The child had the same radiant vitality as Sarah, but with dark hair and eyes.

"Did the stream dry up?" Nellie asked as she stroked the baby's rosy cheek.

Sarah shook her head. "We built a new house. We were married a month after you left." She motioned to someone behind her. Another red-cheeked, dark-eyed baby was carried up the aisle by a tall, dark young man with a well-tanned face.

"I'm so pleased to meet you," Nellie said, shaking the young man's hand.

"You might as well meet the whole family at once," Sarah went on. Then she snapped her fingers over her shoulder, and Nellie felt she was in a dream when two little boys started coming up the aisle, dressed alike in Red River overcoats. Their identical blond curls showed under their blue caps.

"Meet the troops," Sarah said, and the two blue caps were removed from the blond heads. "George and Dan are three, and the girls are ten months old. We came in to Winnipeg to show you how we are prospering. You know it's been almost five years since I last saw you."

"Two sets of identical twins!" Nellie exclaimed. "Four beautiful children — so soon. You've hardly been married five years and already you have your family!"

"That's what you think," said Sarah. Nellie raised her eyebrows in question but did not ask further. Sarah's husband was beaming proudly at his young family.

"I'd like to stay," Sarah said finally, "but we're driving home tonight. We just bought a car, and when I read in the paper that you were speaking, I knew we had to get here!"

Nellie gave Sarah a hug and made her way over to Wes.

Nellie's arm rested on Wes's as they walked from their garage to the house. Inside the kitchen, she put the tea kettle on to boil, threw her coat on the old, striped couch, and sank into her rocking chair. The house was completely quiet — Alice and the children were all asleep.

Wes sat on the couch and reached over to take Nellie's hand. "You look tired tonight, Nell," he said. "This last round of speeches has been too much, I think. Two weeks is a long time."

"Yes, I've surely missed you — but I've had some exciting times, Wes."

"Nell, I'm glad you're home now. I've taken a few days off work, so we'll have some free time together."

"I'll love that, Wes, and remember — Florence's big birthday party is on Wednesday. Oh, I *am* glad to be home — though I do like my work."

"I understand," Wes said.

"I was only sixteen when I got my eyes on you, Wes, but I knew what I was doing!" She leaned over and took his big hand in her small one and squeezed it.

They were interrupted by a loud knocking on the front door. Wes took the watch out of the breast pocket of his vest and looked at the time. "It's eleven o'clock. Who on earth can that be now!"

He got up slowly and went to the front door. Five women fairly tumbled in out of the snow.

"Oh, Nellie, we've plans!" said Mrs. Nash as she saw Nellie coming up behind her husband. "We couldn't wait any longer to tell you!"

Nellie wondered what they could possibly be thinking of as she took the women's coats and offered them chairs in the sitting room.

"It was all Lillian's idea," Mrs. Nash began. "I'll let her tell you."

"Well, I was in Vancouver, and I heard about a skit put on by the University Women's Club there," said Lillian Thomas. "Women assumed the places held now by men, and men were the voteless sex, dependent on the chivalry of women, and not liking it any too well."

"So we all got to work on it," said Mrs. Graham, "and do we have plans now!"

"First," said Mrs. Nash, "we are going to go as a delegation to the Legislative Assembly, to ask for the vote. Sir Rodmond will, of course, refuse."

"The delegation will go on Tuesday afternoon, January twenty-seventh. Then on Wednesday evening, we'll put our play on at the Walker Theatre. We're going to call it *The Women's Parliament*. It'll be a replica of the Legislative Assembly of Manitoba — made up entirely of women. Only women are going to be voters and only women will sit in parliament."

"We start rehearsing at the theatre at nine tomorrow morning — before their regular performances," said Lillian.

"I'll enjoy watching that," Nellie laughed.

"Watching!" Mrs. Nash exclaimed. "We want you to play the part of Sir Rodmond."

"Sir Rodmond!"

"Yes, when we go to meet with him on Tuesday, you can observe what he does and says. Then all you have to do is imitate him."

"Excellent!" said Nellie. "Count me in!"

Mrs. Nash and her companions rose to go and tumbled back out into the night — a mass of fur hats and chatter. "I'm too excited to sleep!" Nellie heard Lillian say as the women headed down the sidewalk over the crunching snow.

"*I* certainly won't have any trouble sleeping," Nellie said to Wes as they took each other's hands and headed up the stairs.

16

"What a fine delegation we have here this after-noon!" Sir Rodmond announced with as much gallantry as he could muster. His paunch pro-truded from his pinstriped suit jacket as he rocked back and forth on his heels. "Fine minds but, just as important, fine specimens of womanly beauty. In fact, the speeches we have just been graced with show such refinement and feminine culture that it's clear they are not the product of women's suf-frage.

"These women were brought up in the tradi-tions of our fathers, and their civility and wit only demonstrate how valuable those traditions are."

Nellie, along with the other members of the PEL delegation, was sitting at a long oak table between the two sides of the legislative chamber.

She yearned to take notes but knew she must not. It might make the MPPs suspicious that something was afoot. She listened intently, hoping to capture every word and phrase so she could use them the next night in the Mock Parliament.

"I listened carefully to Mrs. McClung," the premier went on, "and found evidence in every word to prove that men have made sacrifices in order that women might have the culture and accomplishments that have been demonstrated here." Sir Rodmond clasped his hands together with his thumbs straight up, moving them up and down as he thought between sentences.

"Where," he added, "can we get better evidence of woman's superiority and the high place that she occupies than has been given here today?

"Remember that old saying — The hand that rocks the cradle rules the world! You see, women already rule, and so you can achieve no greater status.

"I challenge anyone to produce better evidence of a woman's high place. Now, I could make a speech in favour of women's suffrage —"

Cheers from Mrs. Nash, Lillian Thomas, Claire Graham, and the other women at the oak table interrupted the premier.

". . . *but* I can see reasons that cause me to hesitate . . . . Every good citizen will tell you that a fundamental of national greatness is the home. Because the home lives of our communities and our nation are excellent, we now enjoy the golden opportunities of the twentieth century. Now, does the franchise for women make our homes better?"

Cries of assent followed.

Unruffled, the premier continued, "The facts are against you. It has been said that you want suffrage because it will make society better. But this will not be the case. It will bring about the break-up of the home and, in fact, *divorce!* Now, I am not going to meet some of the arguments that have been submitted here today. Because of the chivalry that my mother inspired in me, I will not embarrass the fine women here by stooping to answer their arguments. The answers to those arguments are so obvious that it would be insulting to present them . . ."

Sir Rodmond ranted on at his foamy best, his stomach still protruding and his arms waving. Government and Opposition MPPs were eyeing him and the women closely. A new silence fell over the House as he spoke — very different from the everyday kind that was caused by the honourable members reading newspapers, dozing off, and waiting for the vote so they could leave for the day.

Nellie strained to lock each phrase and mannerism in her mind. And what a marvelously bumbling speech he was giving her! He was playing right into her hands. She could hardly wait to go home and practise in front of the bedroom mirror.

"In conclusion," Sir Rodmond barked, blowing himself up like a balloon, "I would like to say that I give women my full support to stay as they are! Any civilization that has produced the noble women I see before me is good enough for me. And if it is good enough for *me*, it is good enough for *anybody*." He swept the audience with a penetrating gaze, his brows beetling above his eyes, as if daring anyone to contradict him.

When no one spoke, he continued, "These gentle women, queens of the home, set apart by their great function of motherhood, are superior to men. I revere my dear mother, and for her sweet sake, I reverence all women, I open doors for women, I lift my hat to women. What more could a truly gentle woman want?"

"Justice," Nellie said in a stage whisper that echoed clear across the stately room.

"We went there asking for plain, common justice, an old-fashioned square deal, and what did we get in reply?" Nellie said with disgust.

"A good deal of blarney, I'll bet," said Alice, who had just changed from her college clothes to her work ones.

"How was your meeting with Roblin Redbreast?" said Jack, stumbling down the stairs in his hurry. He was attending classes at Wesley College and had come home for a few days to join in the excitement. He was looking forward to the Mock Parliament and had sold tickets to his classmates and a few of his teachers.

"Roblin said just what we expected he would say, Jack. He said the home would be ruined by voting women. Then he went on with the usual stuff — but he gave me all the right lines for tomorrow night's speech."

The back door opened and Wes stomped in, shaking snow out of his hair and unbuttoning his

Red River coat. He'd just been down to the curling rink to check on the hours. After supper, he planned to take Florence and her two best friends there as part of her birthday present. The other half of her present would be acting as a page in the Mock Parliament.

The big party had been cancelled.

Florence had been terribly upset when Nellie told her. Her birthday coincided with the night of the big performance, and every ounce of Nellie's energy had to go toward preparing for it. Wes and Nellie hoped that having a surprise visit to the curling rink a day early would help soften their daughter's disappointment.

"Well, I made the arrangements at the rink," said Wes. "I hope the surprise will help Florence get over not having a party. By the way, where *is* Florence?"

"At the library. Horace wanted a book for his project, and Mark begged to go too. So Florence took them both right after school. They should be home any time."

"Good! And is supper ready?" Wes boomed. "I could use a great big venison steak right this minute."

"You're such a carnivore, Wes."

"That I am — but at least I'm good at stocking up on the meat I want to eat!"

"That's true. There's so much meat in the icebox there's hardly space for anything else — even though I fed half of it to the neighbour's dog on Saturday."

"You what?"

"It wasn't fresh anymore, Wes. And we couldn't possibly have eaten that much in the next few days."

"You could have invited the neighbours in instead of fattening up their dog! You're always inviting people over for meals. What gave you cold feet this time?"

"Don't talk to me about cold feet right now, Wes. I already have cold feet."

"Why, Nellie?" Wes asked, softening a bit.

"Well, I'm scared now. I'm playing Roblin in the Mock Parliament tomorrow — and it's got to be just right. The fate of the women of Manitoba hangs on my every word."

"Oh, Nell. You'll do just fine. You always do." Wes sounded more distant than usual.

"What's the matter, Wes?"

"I hope you at least kept the rest of the venison."

"Yes, I kept the venison . . . and guess what? We're having a roast tonight!"

"All right, then. I declare a truce. But next time, let me know before you clear out the icebox, will you?"

Just then Florence burst in through the back door. Her fur muff was dangling from her shoulder, and her hat was hanging sideways on her head.

"Call the police!" she shouted breathlessly. "The boys have disappeared. I looked everywhere and asked everyone at the library. There's no trace of Horace and Mark. We searched the grounds. There were snowtracks in the yard. It looked like a tussle of some kind had gone on." Florence was so frantic that her breath was coming in fast, rattling gulps. She fell into the nearest chair without taking her boots off. Puddles of melting snow started to form around them.

"I really can't believe anyone would kidnap the boys — right out of the library," Wes said. "Now, Florence, you tell us *exactly* what happened."

"Mark was getting restless and wanted to go outside to play. Horace said he'd watch him. You know, Horace is always good with him."

"Yes, I know," said Nellie in a calm voice, but her breath was catching as she thought of what might have happened to them.

"Well, there was only about five minutes left of the puppet show. They were getting bored, so I dressed them up and told them to stay near the doorway and I'd be out soon to walk them home. I didn't want to leave right away because the librarian is a friend of mine. She'd asked to speak to me right afterwards."

"Well, that's a busy area and safe too. No one would touch them. So stop your worrying. They probably wandered off with one of Horace's friends," said Wes.

Nellie put her hands in her apron pockets to stop them from shaking. Like Florence, she was preparing herself for the worst, but Wes's strong, reassuring tones were keeping her from panic. Silently she prayed for God to protect her boys.

There came a loud banging sound at the back door. Nellie rushed over and struggled to open it. As she fumbled with the latch in her anxiety, the door suddenly gave way. Horace and Mark almost fell into the room.

Hatless, Horace was still clutching his three-year-old brother's little mittened hand. Mark's bright eyes were sparkling, but his toque hung off the back of his head. His clothes were torn, and snow covered his blond curls. His cheeks glowed like red apples.

Nellie stared at her two youngest boys almost speechless. "Wherever have you been?" she asked. "What happened to you?"

"Well, Mark ran outside," Horace began, "so Florence said I could watch him out there. He got in a fight with some other kids. They threw snowballs and knocked off his hat. Then I fought the other kids. Then Mark got into it too. We both looked so dirty and ragged I didn't want to go back in the library."

"Horace, how could you run away like that and not tell Florence where you'd gone?" Wes had his hand on Horace's shoulder and was speaking firmly and staring into Horace's upturned eyes.

Horace's lip quivered as he said, "I just forgot. I forgot!" Then he added, "I brought us home the long way, by the back lanes. I was afraid a reporter from the *Telegram* would see us and take a picture."

Wes's eyes started to twinkle and he looked over at Nellie.

"Can't you just see the headlines in the paper?" Horace continued in a tone of scorn, "Nellie McClung's Neglected Children. Can't you see? I couldn't do anything else."

Nellie and Wes looked at each other, then over at the exhausted Florence, still in her coat and boots. "It's all right, Florence, don't you worry," said Nellie. "You didn't do anything wrong."

Then she knelt down and put her arms around Horace. "You don't need to be concerned about the press, Horace. I can take care of them. But I love you for what you did."

"Well, *I* don't," Florence shouted. She bolted out of the chair she had collapsed into a few minutes before. "How could you *do* such a thing, Horace? How *could* you? I was worried *sick*, I was! But little did you care!"

"Now, Florence, calm down," said Wes, coming over to stand beside her.

"I won't calm down. I won't! And I know about your stupid curling surpise. My friend Dianne thought I knew, so I found out when she told me. But I don't want to go. It's not the same as a real party. And it's not my birthday today anyway. I wanted a party *tomorrow*! Mother, you promised! And then you broke your promise at almost the last minute. I always come *last* around here. Almost anything and anyone else comes first! Why can't I belong to a *normal* family?" Florence ran from the room, tearing off her hat and coat as she went.

Nellie and Wes stared at each other in silence as Florence pounded up the stairs. They both flinched as a door slammed above them.

Then the back door opened. This time it was Paul. "Everyone looks like they've been struck by lightening. What's the matter?" he asked, hanging his skates on a nail by the door and walking into the pantry. "Anything to eat? It's almost supper time!"

Alice came to life then, "Oh, my, I'm sorry, Mrs.

McClung, but it won't be long now. Just let me through to the pantry. I'll have it ready in no time at all."

A silence hung heavy over the McClung household as the evening meal drew to a close. "Is it all right if I take Florence up a plateful?" Alice asked.

"Yes, but leave the cake," Nellie said. "I want to take that up later."

"Ah, Ma, aren't we going to get a piece?" Paul asked.

"Maybe later," said Nellie. "But not now. Florence gets the first one."

"The cake may be stale by then," Paul grumbled.

After the meal was cleared, Nellie went into the study to write out her script for the next night's performance. But she could not concentrate. She looked at her watch. Florence had had time to finish her first helping. So it was time to take up the cake. It was a beautiful three-layer, chocolate birthday cake that she'd decorated herself.

As Nellie walked into her daughter's bedroom, Florence turned her tear-stained face toward her. Nellie swallowed as she sat down beside her daughter and held out the cake with its fifteen flaming candles.

A little smile twitched at the corners of Florence's mouth. Nellie was glad to see that she was calmer now. But would Florence make a wish? Too many of Florence's wishes had been dashed lately, it seemed.

"What shall I wish for?" Florence mumbled to

herself with a sigh. Then she said, "I know. Mother, I wish that when I'm twenty-one, I'll be allowed to vote."

Nellie looked at her daughter with relief. The storm had passed.

"You might just get that wish," said Nellie. "We have six years to work on it!" Nellie set down the two blue-willow plates she'd brought upstairs and cut two huge pieces of cake.

Florence took hers without saying anything. Nellie pulled a chair up next to the bed and started eating.

"This isn't too bad, Mother," said Florence through a mouthful of chocolate.

"Thank you, dear. I decorated it, but Alice made it. Now she's busy sewing your page costume for the Mock Parliament."

"Oh, yes, I forgot."

"It's almost ready to try on."

"Oh, is it?" Florence tried not to show her enthusiasm but did not entirely succeed.

"Alice was hemming the cuffs on the jacket just before supper. It has snappy brass buttons and gold braid — just like a real page outfit."

"We'll be the first women in parliament, won't we?"

"Yes, we're making history tomorrow night, Florence."

"Maybe someday women will be allowed to run for office in a *real* parliament!"

"I hope so, Florence, but first we have to win the vote!"

17

"Roblin, Roblin Redbreast
O-oh Roblin dear,
It was the tongue of Nellie McClung
That spoiled your taste for beer."

Nellie and Florence pushed their way past the crowds that were already lining up for last-minute tickets outside the Walker Theatre. The would-be audience was keeping warm by stamping their feet and singing political songs.

"Lining up for the Old Maids' Convention?" a passerby yelled at the assembled multitude, but no one responded. They were too caught up in the excitement of the moment.

They also took no notice of a man in a raccoon coat who advised his wife, "No, dear, that's not for us. Just a lot of clap-trap trumped up by short-haired women and long-haired men."

Half an hour later, crowds poured into the foyer of the theatre, where they were asked to sign a suffrage petition to the government. Many of them did. Mr. Babcock and his fellow Liberal Party workers were walking up and down the aisles, selling Dr. Mary Crawford's pamphlet, "The Legal Status of Women in Manitoba."

Nellie was standing behind the big asbestos curtain, thrilled at the sight of the huge audience. The Walker Theatre was crammed to the roof.

"Don't spare him, Nellie," Mrs. Nash said, coming up behind her and squeezing her hand. "We've tried the reasonable way, but Sir Rodmond is blind and cannot be moved. This is a play — but a deadly serious one!"

Nellie let go of Mrs. Nash's hand and strode out in front of the curtain. As soon as the spotlight fell on her, the audience burst into a round of uproarious applause. They had recognized her instantly.

"Ladies and gentlemen, you will have to use your imagination as you watch this play," she advised the audience. "Political conditions are reversed and women are in power. Some people have been known to object to the idea of having women work as politicians. But I don't see why they should not sit in parliament. It doesn't seem to be such a hard job!"

Gales of laughter followed.

"And just to make sure our play was authentic, we visited the legislature yesterday to get some local colour."

Louder laughter filled the auditorium.

Nellie disappeared and the curtain rose, revealing the women legislators, dressed in evening gowns covered with black cloaks, seated at their desks, ready for the first session.

Mrs. Graham, playing the part of the Speaker of the House, sat on a throne, wearing a purple velvet cape and a three-cornered hat with a sweeping white plume. The two pages, played by Florence and a friend, Ruth Walker, were delivering newspapers and personal telephone messages for the MPPs. Mrs. Nash, playing a Conservative cabinet minister, filed her nails and ate chocolates. Lillian Thomas, as leader of His Majesty's Loyal Opposition, spent an enormous amount of time powdering her nose. Dr. Mary Crawford, as the Liberal member for the Northwest, buried herself in a copy of the *Telegram.*

The first petition from a public delegation was received and read. It was a protest against men's clothes, saying that men wearing scarlet ties, six-inch collars, and squeaky shoes should not be allowed in public. The next one asked that all injurious substances be prohibited in the manufacture of laundry soap as it ruined men's delicate hands.

Lillian Thomas, as leader of the Opposition, rose to present a bill. "I request," she said, directing her gaze hopefully from side to side of the House, "that we give the father equal guardianship rights with the mother."

She hesitated and looked around at the Honourable Members. Dr. Mary Crawford stood up and waved her hand — but she was only signalling

Florence to bring her a cup of coffee. Florence sailed across the room, carrying a real china cup on a tray above her head.

"Why are you taking this stand?" shouted Mrs. Nash, the Conservative cabinet minister. "It seems to me that you want to stand in well with the men!"

Titters of laughter rippled through the House. There was a loud pounding of desks. The leader of the Opposition turned bright red with the help of a light flashing on her face from offstage.

"Let us not waste more time on this matter," said the Speaker of the House, the plume of her hat waving noticeably. "We will put it to the vote!"

The House divided along party lines, with the government members yawning loudly and shouting, "No!"

Then Dr. Mary Crawford, Liberal member for Northwest, stood up to present the bill. "I believe that men should have dower rights," she announced. "Does the working man not devote his life to his wife and family? Yet at the present time, he has no voice in the disposition of his property. His wife can sell it over his head or will it away. In fact, this has been done —"

"I myself am keen on men," cut in the sarcastic voice of Mrs. Nash, Conservative cabinet minister, with the true composure of a real statesman. "But do you think that, when left on their own, the wife and mother will not deal fairly with the husband? Surely the wife would not want the iron hand of the law to intrude in her home? Do you dare to imply that love has to be upheld by the law? Did not a man at the altar, in the sight of God and witnesses, endow his wife with all his goods?

"Well, then, are those sacred words to be blasphemed by an unholy law which compels the wife to give back what her husband has so lovingly given? When a man marries, he gives his wife his name, his heart, his property, and his goods, and he gives them unconditionally. Who are we to meddle with these gifts of love?"

Desks were being thumped behind the Conservative cabinet minister. She continued, "The Opposition is guilty of a gross offence against good taste in opening up this question again. It is positively indecent!"

The Honourable Member from Northwest begged leave to withdraw her motion.

The MPPs' afternoon snooze was then interrupted again, this time by the appearance of Mr. Babcock. He was leading a deputation of men pushing wheelbarrows full of petitions for "votes for men."

Representatives from both sides of the House laughed hilariously. A delegation of men seemed to be a long-standing joke.

"I move that they be heard," said one member. "It's been a dull afternoon. We need a little . . . ahem . . . diversion." The House was resolved into a committee of the whole, with the premier at the front.

As the premier rose to speak, many spectators raised their opera glasses. Under the grey wig, the face they saw was unmistakably that of Nellie McClung. They chuckled, knowing they would see a good performance. Her well-known sharp, brown eyes were snapping, but she greeted the delegation with a pleasant smile.

Behind the premier, the members of her government gazed down at the men with amused tolerance.

"What a fine delegation of men we have here this afternoon!" the premier began. "Gentlemen, I am glad to see you. Come anytime and ask for anything you like. You are just as welcome this time as you were the last time! In fact, we like delegations, and I congratulate you on your splendid gentlemanly manners. And, furthermore, what fine specimens of manly beauty you are."

Ripples of laughter spread through the audience. Many of them had obviously read the premier's speech in that morning's *Telegram.*

Then Nellie clasped her hands in front of her, locking her fingers with the thumbs straight up. It was the premier's own gesture, and more howls of recognition came from the audience.

"Madam," began Mr. Babcock, their leader, "we have come yet again to request that men be given the privilege of voting. We have summarized our request in this motto — We have the brains. Why not let us vote?"

Nellie waited for silence before she spoke. "Now, you also have a fine leader. In fact, I can tell that all of you come from cultured families. But, unfortunately, not all men are of the same intellectual capacity. In fact, few are of the same intellect and culture. You, Mr. Babcock, with the customary hot-headedness of a reformer, have not stopped to think of that. Where men have the vote, it has been shown that men make up seven-eighths of the Police Court offenders and only one-third of the church membership."

The audience broke out into gales of laughter again. Nellie was tempted to laugh with them, but she succeeded in keeping a serious expression on her face.

Just as things were settling down, Nellie stuck out her stomach and teetered back and forth on her heels exactly the way the premier did. The spectators roared with laughter, but Nellie's facial expression never changed. She was apparently deaf to her audience.

When silence finally fell, Nellie's voice, a throaty contralto, was marked by a cordial paternalism. "Another trouble is that if men start to vote, they will vote too much. Politics unsettles men, and unsettled men mean unsettled homes — broken furniture, broken vows and — divorce!" The premier's voice was heavy with sorrow now, for having mentioned anything so unpleasant.

Laughter burst forth again and Nellie had to stop talking. People were slapping their knees, and loud guffaws were rising from the audience. The men were laughing as hard as the women.

Then the premier's mood seemed to change. She spoke in the loud, ringing voice of one who is leading others to their highest destiny. "Man has a higher aim than politics," she cried. "What is a home without a bank account? The man who pays the grocer rules the world. Shall I call men away from the useful plough and harrow, to talk aloud on the street corners about things which do not concern them? Ah, no, I love the farm and the hallowed associations — the dear old farm with the drowsy tinkle of cowbells at eventide. There I see my father's kindly smile so full of blessing. A hard-working, rough-handed man he was, but able to look the whole world in the face. You ask me to change all this?"

Nellie's voice shook with emotion and, drawing a huge white linen handkerchief from the folds of her gown, she held it by the corner, cracked it like a whip, and blew her nose like a trumpet.

It seemed then that everyone in the audience caved in at once. The laughter and pounding of feet was ear-splitting.

But the premier had not finished. "Do you never read, gentlemen?" she asked the delegation with biting sarcasm. "Do you not know of the disgraceful happenings in other countries cursed by manhood suffrage? Do you not know that men are creatures of habit?"

"But, sir," burst out Mr. Babcock, "the polls are only open once in four years. It'd be pretty hard to form a habit."

"As I said, when they once get the habit, who knows where it will lead! It is hard enough to keep men at home now. History is full of unhappy examples of men in public life — Nero, Herod, King John. Politics has a blighting, demoralizing effect on men. It dominates them, hypnotizes them, pursues them even after their earthly career is over. Time and again it has been proven that men have come back and voted — even after they were dead!"

The audience gasped at that — for in the

premier's own riding, there were names on the voters' lists, taken, it was alleged, from the tombstones.

Nellie's voice rang out in awe-stricken tones.
"Do you ask me to disturb the sacred calm of our
cemeteries?" Her eyes opened wide at the horror
of the thought. "We are doing very well just as we
are, very well indeed. Women are the best students of political economy. We look very closely at
every dollar of public money to see if we couldn't
make better use of it ourselves before we spend it.
We run our elections as cheaply as they are run
anywhere. We always endeavour to get the greatest
number of votes for the least possible amount of
money. That is political economy."

A voice rose from the Opposition. "But,
madam, I do not agree —"

"How dare you?" The premier's voice darkened.
The spotlight shone on her. Her eyebrows came
down suddenly, the veins in her neck seemed to
swell, and a fury of words broke from her as she
advanced threateningly on the unhappy member.
"You think you can instruct a person older than
yourself, do you? You — with the brains of a but-
terfly, the insight of a bat, the backbone of a jelly-
fish! I was managing governments when you were
still in your highchair! And you dare to tell me
how a government should be run!"

Walking up and down with her hands at right
angles to her body, she stormed and blustered,
turning eyes of rage on the audience, who were
now rolling in their seats with laughter.

"But I must not lose my temper," she said, calm-
ing herself and letting her voice drop, "and I

never do — never — except when I feel like it. If it were not for my extreme modesty, which has on more than one occasion almost blighted my career, I would say that I believe I have been a leader, a factor in building up this fair province; I would say that I believe I have written my name large across the face of this province."

The government supporters applauded loudly.

"I am building a glorious future, where women will rule and men will know their places. For example," the premier went on, "look at these two fine young pages. I suppose, gentlemen of the delegation, that you would have me force young *men* to do their work — when we all know that they are much too excitable, as all men are, and not suited to the demands of parliamentary service. This is through no fault of their own, I might add. It is just the way God made them."

Florence and Ruth stood up straighter to show their superiority.

"But, gentlemen, in spite of your cleverly worded speeches, I will go on just as I have been doing, without the help so generously offered. My wish for this fair, flower-decked land is that I may long be spared to guide its destiny in world affairs. I know there is no one but me to lead these lambs confidently." Her arms spread out to encompass the whole House of women.

"We are not worrying about the coming election. We rest in confidence of the result and will proudly unfurl as we have these many years, the same old banner of the grand old party that has gone down many times to disgrace, but thank God, never to defeat!"

The curtain fell as the last word was spoken, but lifted again to show the House standing, in their evening gowns. A great clapping followed, and the audience rose to their feet in a mighty wave.

A huge bouquet of red roses was handed to Nellie. It was rumoured that they were from two members of the Conservative Party who secretly supported votes for women. As Nellie looked out into the crowd, she saw two men leaving from the back rows.

Everyone else was still on their feet, giving Nellie the loudest, longest standing ovation she had ever received. Right in front, she could see Wes, smiling and clapping harder than all the rest.

18

"I can see it already," said Jack. "Nellie McClung, great woman orator, the Canadian Joan of Arc. Roblin Redbreast will be hopping mad when he reads that on the front pages of the *Free Press* and the *Telegram* tomorrow!"

"You did it up grand tonight, Nell. You stole the show!" said Mrs. Nash, helping herself to a couple of chocolate squares.

Most of the organizers and actresses had left the cast party at 97 Chestnut Street, but Lillian Thomas and Mrs. Nash had stayed later than the rest. Lillian had kicked off her tight satin shoes and stretched out on the sofa. Mrs. Nash was sitting in a wing chair on one side of the fireplace; Nellie and Wes were sitting on the opposite side. Jack, Florence, and Paul were wandering between the sitting room and the dining room, still sampling all the baked delights.

"You really had them mesmerized tonight, Nellie," said Lillian. "Those who didn't sign the petition on the way in were signing it as they came out — and with a smile, I might add."

"Everyone was fantastic — including you, Florence," Nellie replied. "I fear I may have led you astray — into the life of an actress. Promise me you'll finish school first!"

"Oh, Mother, I don't want to be an actress! I want to go to Agricultural College and study domestic science. But I do want to vote. Do you think we'll get the vote soon now, since we were such a success?"

"I hope so. Some men, however, are quite willing to let women entertain them, but are afraid of women who show they are serious about opposing injustice."

"But that works against men, too, doesn't it, Mother?" said Paul as he whisked a macaroon off a nearby plate.

"Yes, it does, but people are slow to change. I think that at the end of their days, many people will look back at their lives and regret not so much what they did as what they did not do. Sometimes it's so hard to move folks to action."

"Well, that certainly won't be said of you, Nellie," Wes laughed.

"Do you think the premier was there tonight?" said Jack.

"I don't know," Nellie said, "but I heard a rumour that someone looking very much like him in profile and wearing dark glasses was seen leaving the auditorium at a fast gait just before the end of the show!"

"It must have been him! The premier saw our play!" Florence shouted.

"But do you think we'll actually succeed in changing his mind?" Mrs. Nash asked.

"Well, if we don't change his mind, we'll just have to change the premier!" said Nellie.

"And we have a chance of doing that," said Lillian. "We got so many signatures tonight, I'm sure public opinion is coming over to our side."

"Yes, and we'll get even more names," said Nellie. "Did you know that a petition with 39,584 names came in last week? And the Liberal Party has been so impressed with our results that they made women's suffrage a part of their platform. T.C. Norris has kept his word to me, and I have faith that he'll follow through."

The clock struck one.

"One o'clock already!" Mrs. Nash exclaimed. "I must go home to my husband."

"And I have to be at the *Press* at eight o'clock tomorrow morning!" said Lillian, regretfully undraping herself from the sofa.

"It's time for *all* of us to go to bed," said Nellie, looking at Florence and Paul.

"But we're wide awake now," said Paul. "Can't we stay up all night?"

Wes and Nellie sat alone on the kitchen couch, listening to the night sounds of the house. The grandfather clock ticked reassuringly from the front hallway and the walls creaked slightly under the pressure of the freezing January wind.

"Do you remember that cold January day when your mother came over and forced me to write the first chapter of *Sowing Seeds in Danny*?" Nellie asked.

"How could I forget it? I had a welcome taste of my own mother's home cooking that night."

"Wes! You scoundrel!"

"I know what you're going to say. We've come a long way since then, haven't we? And it's true."

"Yes, we have, but do you regret having a wife who's so busy outside the home?"

"I do miss you terribly when you're away. And it's especially hard when you go on a long stretch of speaking engagements. But we're fortunate to be living in an age when things are changing for the better in so many ways."

"Yes, we live in the land of the second chance."

"Sir Wilfrid Laurier called this Canada's Century, and I believe it is."

"But there is one dark cloud on the horizon, Nell."

"You mean Germany? The Kaiser?"

"Yes. He's gaining power and there are rumours of war. Germany could become a threat."

Nellie stared into the black night outside the kitchen window. "The army takes boys at eighteen, don't they?" she said.

"Yes, they do," Wes replied.

"And Jack will be seventeen in June . . ."

Wes looked gravely down at his wife and said,

"You know, Nellie, if Britain is at war, it will involve the Empire. It always does."

Then to Wes's surprise, Nellie started to smile.

"Do you remember when the Second Boer War began and all the folks went down to the train station to see the fellows off?"

"I can't say that I do. I guess I was too busy with the drugstore."

"Well, I went down, and I bumped into Mrs. Smith. As the train chugged its way out of the station, she said to me, 'There should be a law to stop a man who has eight children from going. But what can a woman do but just take what comes? He'll be a hero and I'll just be a drudge with bunions on my feet.'"

"Yes, I remember now. You told me that story when you came home. And Mr. Smith *did* become a hero! He won a medal, I believe."

"Yes, he did . . . but back to our own battles," said Nellie. "You know, Wes, we'll still have a tough fight ahead of us. Getting the vote will not be automatic, even if we do have thousands of signatures. Many of the people of Manitoba belong to the old school, like Sir Rodmond. They're conservative by nature and, I'm afraid, Conservative by politics. Our only hope is with the Liberal Party, so we'll campaign for them. But it'll be the fight of our lives!"

"Oh, don't worry, Nellie. It's only a matter of time. Pressure has become so great that women *will* win. One party or the other will *have* to give women the vote. Any party that wants to remain popular will recognize that!"

"I hope you're right. But, Wes, I discovered

something in my research that brings up a whole new problem."

"You did?"

"Yes, the problem is this — there's still an old law on the books that says women are not persons."

"I never heard of it."

"Few people have, but it's there all right. It's in the common law of England, enacted about forty years ago, in 1876. At that time, a brave woman in England decided to vote. So she went out on election day and persuaded the poll clerk to give her a ballot, and she voted!"

"That must have created a reaction!"

"It did! She was arrested for the misdemeanour and tried in court, and that resulted in a ruling on the matter. 'Women,' they said, 'are persons in matters of pains and penalties, but are not persons in matters of rights and privileges.'"

"And as part of the British Empire, we will have inherited that law," said Wes. He sat in shocked silence.

"Well, something has to be done about it," said Nellie.

Wes smiled knowingly at his wife. "And you'll be in the middle of that battle next, won't you?"

Nellie nodded, and with a faraway look in her eye, she said, "Yes, Wes, I *know* I will be."

Epilogue

Although the voters did return Roblin and his government to power the following July, in 1915 a scandal in connection with the building of the new legislature in Winnipeg caused him and his party to resign. During the following election, in August 1915, the Liberals achieved a landslide victory. Meanwhile, the suffrage workers had obtained far more than the designated number of signatures for their cause, so they persuaded the government that the people of Manitoba truly wanted women to have the vote. One petition contained 39,584 names; another contained 4,250 names. Amazingly, the names on the second petition had all been collected by a ninety-four-year-old woman from rural Manitoba. On January 29, 1916, the Manitoba legislature unanimously passed a bill enabling women to vote and run for office in the province, thus becoming the first province in Canada to do this.

Between 1916 and 1940, the other provinces followed Manitoba's lead, and the federal House of Commons granted these rights to Canadian women in 1918. The prairie provinces of Saskatchewan and Alberta followed Manitoba by giving the vote to women in 1916. British Columbia was the fourth in line on April 5, 1917. Ontario was one week later. Nova Scotia followed in 1918, one month after the federal government gave complete enfranchisement. New Brunswick was next in 1919, then Prince Edward Island in 1922. Quebec did not grant this right to women until 1940. Newfoundland, joining the Dominion in 1949, had already given the right to vote in 1925. All provinces except Ontario and New Brunswick gave women the right to hold office in the same year as the right to vote. Ontario granted this privilege in 1919 and New Brunswick in 1934.

In 1914, the McClungs moved to Edmonton, where Nellie was elected a Liberal member of the Alberta Legislature in 1921. Nellie was not the first woman to sit in the Alberta Legislative Assembly, but she was nearly the first. (Mrs. Louise McKinney, elected in 1917, had preceded her; she was the first female member of *any* Legislative Assembly in the British Empire.) Nellie travelled to twenty states in the U.S., advocating for women's suffrage, and drew large, enthusiastic crowds. This too was in 1917. In 1921, Nellie also gained popularity as a speaker at the Methodist

Ecumenical Conference in Britain, where she was the only woman delegate from Canada.

Back in the Alberta Legislature, Nellie continued to fight against the sale of liquor, a position that naturally made her unpopular with the Alberta Hotelkeepers' Association. During the election of 1926, they warned her that they would do everything to make her lose her seat if she did not stop attacking liquor sales. Of course, Nellie did not stop fighting, so she lost the election. Another factor in her defeat was her move from Edmonton to Calgary.

Nellie is perhaps best remembered for her part in the struggle to have women defined as "persons" under the law. Because women in Canada did not always have the rights and privileges of persons, they were left vulnerable to many injustices. When a woman married, for example, her property automatically became her husband's, to do with as he pleased. (The husband, however, kept full rights to his own property.) Nellie joined Emily Murphy, Magistrate for the Province of Alberta (the first female police magistrate in the British Empire), Henrietta Muir Edwards, Louise McKinney, and Irene Parlby in sending a petition to the Supreme Court of Canada concerning this matter, and the appointment of females to Canada's Senate. But the Supreme Court confirmed on April 24, 1928, that women were not persons under our constitution, the B.N.A. Act. (Imagine what little chance a woman would have in any court case against a man, when the court and judge based their decisions on this assumption!)

Not to be stopped, the five women launched an appeal to the Privy Council of England. They could not afford the expense of this undertaking themselves, but they persuaded Prime Minister William Lyon Mackenzie King to send the petition along with other business items at the expense of the Canadian government. As a result, on October 18, 1929, the Privy Council declared that the word "persons" included both men and women.

In 1935, the McClungs moved to British Columbia, where Nellie became the first woman to sit on the CBC's Board of Governors, and in 1938, she became a delegate to the League of Nations. She died in 1951 at the age of seventy-seven, and her husband died seven years later.

In the July 1, 1998, special Canada Day issue of *Maclean's* magazine, the one hundred most important Canadians in Canada's history were selected from reader nominations and by an expert panel. On this list, Nellie L. McClung was put in the category of activist and chosen as one of the top ten, where she was the only woman. J.L. Granatstein, author and professor at York University for thirty years, states in the *Maclean's* article that Nellie "was a feminist ahead of her time, even as she believed it was right and proper to be a devoted wife and mother. McClung's greatest achievement was as one of the 'Famous 5,' the women who challenged the Supreme Court of Canada's 1928 decision that women were not 'persons.'"

On October 18, 1999, the seventieth anniversary of the "Persons" Case, the Famous 5 Foundation will present a larger-than-life bronze monument of these nation builders to the citizens of Calgary. On October 18, 2000, an identical monument on Parliament Hill in Ottawa will be presented to the people of Canada. Also, a stamp will be issued in 1999, and hopefully the next year will see the placement of the Famous 5 on the back of our new five-dollar bill.

Nellie Mooney McClung, who did not learn to read until she was ten and who grew up being told to "hush her talk" in the presence of adults, became a famous speaker, novelist, and activist. This is how *The Toronto Star* described her: ". . . Nellie McClung, prairie reformer, suffragette, parliamentarian, author, newspaperwoman, and Canada's leading pioneer feminist, kept right on fighting for women's rights with the cheery battle cry: 'Never retract, never explain, never apologize — get the thing done and let them howl.'"

That, to the great benefit of Canadian women and men today, is exactly what she did!

Notes

Most of the incidents in *Nellie's Victory* are true, but are dramatized and enhanced with fictional detail to bring them to life. This novel is based on Nellie L. McClung's autobiography, *The Stream Runs Fast*, and also draws from her writings, speeches, and news articles about her. Sometimes, I have combined real people into fictitious characters — an example of this is Sarah and a friend of Nellie's who did actually have a third set of identical twins. The main events such as those of the children's birthdates, the publishing of Nellie McClung's books, the petitions and meetings with the government are accurate, but I have slightly changed the dates of minor events.

Also, I have occasionally quoted from *Purple Springs* and *In Times Like These*, from which the

University of Toronto Press has kindly given me permission to quote. In *The Stream Runs Fast*, Nellie L. McClung said the following: "I wrote *Purple Springs*, a novel, in which the struggle for the vote in Manitoba became the background for this, the third and last of my Pearlie stories. It is a work of fiction, but the part relating to the *Women's Parliament* is substantially a matter of history." (117)

The following quotes (which have been included in *Nellie's Victory*) were taken from *The Stream Runs Fast*, unless otherwise noted. Often, I have changed a quote slightly to make it more readable for today's students. In some cases, I have made more significant changes in Nellie's language. These also are indicated below. The numbers in the left column refer to the pages in *Nellie's Victory*.

CHAPTER ONE
13   "Life conspires . . . trifles.": Nellie L. McClung, *The Stream Runs Fast* (Toronto: Thomas Allen, 1945), 75.

CHAPTER TWO
22   "Will you bring Daniel . . . When Jimmy . . . Jimmy and Pearlie . . . The next day . . . began on Danny.": Nellie L. McClung, *Sowing Seeds in Danny* (Toronto: William Briggs, 1908), 19,20.

CHAPTER THREE
25   "her white leghorn . . . Nellie was determined . . . on the eye.": McClung, 58. (quotation and paraphrase)
27   The name of the horse, Jasper, was taken from Bob Chalmers' Memoirs and was given to me in a personal communication from Diana Vodden, a Manitou resident, 23 September, 1998.

27, 28   "She and Wes . . . all in all.": Nellie L. McClung, "An
          Author's Own Story," *Women's Saturday Night*, 25
          January, 1913, in "McClung Papers," in Candace Savage,
          Our Nell, A Scrapbook Biography of Nellie L. McClung
          (Saskatoon: Western Producer Prairie Books, 1979), 44.
          (quotation and paraphrase)

30   "did not confine . . . in public life.": Savage, *Our Nell*, 45.
          (quotation and paraphrase)

31   "henrietta cloth skirts . . . with brooches.": McClung, 66.

32   "chicken, sliced . . . of potatoes.": Based on McClung, 61.

35   "There's often only . . . get to them . . .": Based on
          McClung, 104.

38   "I hereby solemnly . . . in the same.": Frances E. Willard,
          1974 President of the WCTU, in Brian Burrell, *The
          Words We Live By* (Toronto: The Free Press, 1997), 72.

38   "It's only a second-rate . . . and neglect!": Nellie L.
          McClung, "Minding One's Own Business," in "McClung
          Papers," in Savage, *Our Nell*, 210.

38   "It is not so much a woman's . . . (to change) . . . bring-
          ing them into.": Nellie L. McClung, *In Times Like These*
          (Toronto: University of Toronto Press, 1972), 24.

39   "The very best . . . Lord.": Nellie L. McClung, in
          "McClung Papers," in Savage, *Our Nell*, 48.

39   "The woman who . . . their chance too.": McClung, in
          "McClung Papers," in Savage, *Our Nell*, 48.

39   "I know why people . . . excitement and change.":
          McClung, 58,59.

40   "Prohibition is a hard . . . without your supper.":
          McClung, 59.

41   "Look at the Salvation Army . . . fire with fire.":
          McClung, 59. (quotation and paraphrase).

41   "We can have recreation . . . a new world.": McClung,
          59,60.

41   "Gladstone, once said . . . a sober England.": Based on
          McClung, 62

41   "I believe God (did) . . . destroy us.": McClung, *In Times
          Like These*, 34,35.

41   "From plague . . . deliver us!": McClung, *In Times Like
          These*, 34,35.

42   "the power of speech . . .": McClung, 61.
42   "committed to . . . a hard one.": McClung, 61.

CHAPTER FOUR
43   "delightful story . . . originality.": McClung, 76.
45   "Women were made . . . rival us!": Nellie L. McClung,
            Purple Springs (Toronto: Thomas Allen, 1921), 155.
46   "The man made . . . grain trade . . .": Randi R. Warne,
            "Introduction," in *Purple Springs,* by Nellie L. McClung
            (Toronto: University of Toronto Press, 1992), xxi, xxii.
46   "the woman's movement . . . going downhill.": Warne,
            "Introduction," in *Purple Springs,* 1992, xxi, xxii.
48   "He did not often . . . became helpless.": Charles Oke,
            "McCreary Man Recalls Kindness of Nellie McClung,"
            Western Producer, 17 January, 1974, in Savage, *Our Nell,*
            51. (paraphrase)
50   "When you have . . . where you be.": McClung, 29.

CHAPTER FIVE
66, 67   "little things . . . We are . . . pledged to fight.": Nellie L.
            McClung, Carman, Manitoba WCTU Convention
            Speech, 1910, in "McClung Papers," in Savage, *Our Nell,*
            47,48. (quotation and paraphrase)
67   "But WCTU women . . . four walls.": "WCTU
            Convention," *Grain Grower's Guide,* 17 May, 1911, 25,26,
            in Savage, *Our Nell,* 48. (quotation and paraphrase)
68   "Association has appealed . . . run by women!": Based on
            McClung, 63.
72   "I could tell her . . . little of her.": Jack McClung, in
            McClung, 29.
72   "I stepped on . . . and Ben did.": McClung, 29.
76   "I never did . . . spotted lily.": Wes McClung, in
            McClung, 90.

CHAPTER SIX
83   "Tonight at home . . . touches of humour.": E.S. Caswell,
            in "McClung Papers," in Savage, *Our Nell,* 56.
84   "never refused if a trustworthy person . . .": Based on
            McClung, 40.

85   "Dr. Barner, brilliant . . . and forgotten.": McClung,
          Sowing Seeds in Danny, 30,31.
85   "a red-faced . . . mellow exhilaration.": McClung, *Sowing
          Seeds in Danny*, 36.
91, 92   "Yes! First I went . . . Then I told . . . Wes looked . . .
          Then I came home . . . her husband.": Based on
          McClung, 90,91.

CHAPTER SEVEN

96   "thick, lead-coloured . . . western horizon.": McClung,
          Purple Springs (1921), 1.
97   "the Klondike heaters . . . diligently tending . . .":
          McClung, 28.
98   "The Watson family . . . into a book.": McClung, 76.
          (quotation and paraphrase)
100   "You must look . . . Oh Wes . . . An intelligent . . . But,
          Wes . . . else to do it?": Mark McClung, "The Incredible
          Nellie McClung," interview by Florence Bird, *Between
          Ourselves*, C.B.C. Radio, 6 June, 1975, in Savage, *Our Nell*,
          44.
100   Wes's overspending on meat is based on Miriam Green
          Ellis, "Nellie McClung," *Pathfinders*, Canadian Women's
          Press Club Pamphlet, 14, in Savage, *Our Nell*, 44.
100   "I'd rather quarrel . . . fair fighter!": Nellie L. McClung,
          Clearing in the West (Toronto: Thomas Allen and Son
          Limited, 1965), 374,375.
100   Isaac Watts, *Joy to the World*, 1674-1748.
102   "makes me glad . . . what I know!": in "McClung Papers,"
          in Savage, *Our Nell*, 63.
102, 103 "I am just finishing . . . as in Danny.": Reverend J.A.
          McClung, in a letter to Nellie McClung, 15 November,
          1908, in "McClung Papers," in Savage, *Our Nell*, 62.
103, 104 "Sometimes it is . . . known to slam it!": McClung, *In
          Times Like These*, 10.
104   "terrible meek . . . gentle persuasion.": McClung, 77.
108   "Conservatives passed an order in council . . .":
          McClung, 63.

CHAPTER EIGHT

114	"untidy little places . . . There was no reason . . . provision for everyone.": McClung, 135,136. (paraphrase)
116	"If the insured . . . against death only.": McClung, 112.
116	"Why is it . . . give (a man)?": McClung, 112.
116, 117	"Don't you know . . . no end of trouble.": McClung, 112.
117	"what about the clause . . . could you not?": McClung, 112.
117	"I hope to have . . . Mr. McGregor looked . . . No, but they will.": McClung, 112. (quotation and paraphrase)
119	"female property owners . . . A long-standing right . . . Yes, and since . . . sit on school boards.": Based on Catherine Cleverdon, *The Woman Suffrage Movement in Canada* (Toronto: University of Toronto Press, 1974), 51-53, in Warne, "Introduction," in *Purple Springs*, 1992, xxi.
120	"dinosaurs in the flesh!": Based on "Odds and Ends of the Suffrage Campaign," Lillian Beynon Thomas Papers, Manitoba Archives, in Savage, *Our Nell*, 79, ftn. 30.
120	"Some of our most faithful helpers (are) men.": McClung, 134.
120	"We're in sight of . . . submit to injustice.": McClung, 134. (quotation and paraphrase)
120	"we will never bow . . . supporting it.": Nellie L. McClung, "The Social Responsibilities of Women," typescript of a speech, in "McClung Papers," in Savage, *Our Nell*, 82.
123	"I've thought about . . . do anything else.": McClung, 2. (paraphrase)
123	"the rose-leaf from summer hat!": McClung, 77.
127	"Plough a fireguard.": McClung, *Purple Springs* (1921), 244.
128	"This is a new country . . . are things of the past." Based on McClung, 62.
128	"Submission to oppression is rebellion against God!": McClung, "The Social Responsibilities of Women," in Savage, *Our Nell*, 82.

CHAPTER NINE

129   "Mosquito McClung": Based on McClung, xii.

129, 138   "When (she) awakened . . . She's a big woman . . . Irish,
           you know.": McClung, 127.

130   "Quite a decent . . . Nellie McClung's husband.":
           McClung, 128.

130   "it's only the truth . . . of truth.": McClung, 129,130.

133   "I'm nearing sixty . . . only safe future.": McClung, 79.
           (paraphrase)

134   "She is so . . . will become of her!": McClung, 79.

134   "We have a problem . . . I think ahead.": McClung, 79.

135   "There's a young man . . . and good looking.":
           McClung, 79.

135, 136   "I will not live . . .Mrs. Sayers threw . . . Sarah went on . . .
           Has he children . . . No . . . Don't you think . . . You
           learned everything . . . Oh, Sarah . . . in real distress.":
           McClung, 79,80.

137   "foreshadowing of what women . . . keeping the bal-
           ance.": McClung, 80,81. (paraphrase)

145   "But could it kill . . . kill anyone?": Jack McClung, in
           McClung, 92.

145   "Well, then . . . again, ever?": McClung, 92.

145   "You surely wouldn't . . . stepfathers are like!": McClung,
           92.

145, 146   "There will be no Murdstones . . . we would manage.":
           McClung, 92. (paraphrase)

147   "one of those green . . . in the wind.": McClung, 127.

149   "Good old Wes . . . store's distress.": Jack McClung, in
           McClung, 98.

CHAPTER TEN

150   "If this were a man's . . . long ago.": McClung, 16.

150   "Women have . . . and said nothing.": McClung, 16.
           (paraphrase)

151   "Women must suffer; it keeps them humble!": McClung,
           16.

152   "Tears were not . . . too much already.": McClung, 17.

152   "Women do bear . . . doctors know it.": Dr. MacCharles,
           in McClung, 18.

152 "Medical science . . . infancy.": McClung, 18.

153 "There is neither . . . male or female." and "for you are all one in Christ Jesus.": Galatians 3:28 *The Bible:* King James Version.

154 "have a right to vote . . . citizens!": Based on Warne, "Introduction," in *Purple Springs*, 1992, xix.

154 "Women are weaker . . . made them so.": Premier Roblin, in McClung, *Purple Springs* (1921), 214.

158 "bright June day . . . willow blossoms.": McClung, 99.

CHAPTER ELEVEN

160, 161 "Streetcars wove . . . they were having.": McClung, *Purple Springs* (1921), 301. (quotation and paraphrase)

162 "typhoid fever . . . is not much better.": Based on Savage, *Our Nell*, 68.

164 "Here is a man . . . sign above the door.": Nellie L. McClung, *The Second Chance* (Toronto: The Ryerson Press, 1910) 201.

164, 165 "Everyone of you . . . Let us pray.": McClung, *The Second Chance*, 201,202.

167 "settle down . . . clothed and fed.": McClung, 126.

167 "quite right in saying . . . I hear . . . thought for mine!": McClung, 131.

168 "Children are not . . . his board and keep.": McClung, *In Times Like These*, 22.

168 "what do we mean . . . they are blamed.": Warne, "Introduction," in *Purple Springs*, 1992, xix. (quotation and paraphrase)

168 "It is for this reason . . . moral mothering.": Warne, "Introduction," in *Purple Springs*, 1992, xix. (paraphrase)

168 "The hand that rocks the cradle . . .": McClung, 1914 campaign speech, in "McClung Papers," in Savage, *Our Nell*, 97.

169 "I am a firm . . . the standards high . . .": McClung, in Savage, *Our Nell*, 48.

169 "at home . . . husband's socks.": Based on May L. Armitage, "Mrs. Nellie McClung," *Maclean's*, July 1915, 38, in Savage, *Our Nell*, 98.

CHAPTER TWELVE

170, 171   "early months of . . . Political Equity League.": Based on Warne, "Introduction," in *Purple Springs*, 1992, xxiv.

171   "chicken sandwiches and olives.": McClung, 101.

171   "one thousand people . . . the performance.": Based on Nellie L. McClung, "A Retrospect," *The Country Guide* 3, 2 December, 1929, in Savage, *Our Nell*, 85, ftn. 36.

171   "a florid, rather good-looking . . . sixties.": McClung, 103.

173   "a cut-glass vase . . . carnations . . .": McClung, 102.

173   "With his plump . . . gold-headed . . .": McClung, 103.

173   "As a boy . . . the apple trees.": McClung, 103.

173, 174   "These young factory . . . off the streets.": McClung, 103.

174   "most of the women . . . curse of this age.": McClung, 103.

175   "They all walked . . . outside stairs.": McClung, 103.

175   "airless basement . . . Untidy women . . . sewing machines . . .": McClung, 103.

177, 178   "For God's sake . . . existed!": McClung, 104.

178   "These people work . . . seemed lost on . . .": McClung, 104.

181   "In fact . . . How about the girl . . . built up a bit?": McClung, 105.

181   "The company is not . . . gesture of freedom.": McClung, 105.

182   "Now, Sir Rodmond . . . great opportunities?": McClung, 105.

182   "I still can't see . . . disgusting things.": McClung, 105.

182   "Your factory inspector . . . these places.": McClung, 105.

182   "Why should women . . . concern them?": McClung, 105.

182   "we have no intention . . . social worker.": McClung, 105,106.

183   "I tell you . . . inspector about it.": McClung, 106.

CHAPTER THIRTEEN

184   "a fire burned in a heater, (a canary) sang (in a cage next to a side table and) a cat lay . . .": McClung, *Purple Springs* (1921), 134.

184   "in a pink-and-white-checked . . . French roll.":
        McClung, *Purple Springs* (1921), 134.

185   "Women in Manitoba . . . status of infants!": McClung, in
        Savage, *Our Nell*, 78.

187, 188 "Women in Manitoba . . . his wife's well-being.":
        McClung, in Savage, *Our Nell*, 78.

188–190 "One of them stole . . . It makes you . . . Many women . . .
        A tall, thin . . . This is the chivalry of . . . But a great . . .
        These laws . . . Nellie caught . . . There is also the young
        . . . Class C is . . . The audience . . . Here is an assort-
        ment . . . their case is hopeful.": McClung, "The Social
        Responsibilities of Women," in "McClung Papers," in
        Savage, *Our Nell*, 83-85.

191   "I will tell . . . style about her!": Janey Canuck, "What
        Janey Thinks of Nellie," interviewed by Emily F. Murphy,
        Maclean's, 35, 1 September, 1921, in Savage, *Our Nell*,
        66, ftn. 4.

192   "You'll make a fine . . . Eight! I'd sooner . . . not at
        home!": Based on McClung, 30,31.

193   "any woman . . . home to do it!": Nellie L. McClung,
        "Woman on the War Path," *Maclean's*, January 1929, in
        Savage, *Our Nell*, 98, ftn. 23.

193, 194 "And I'm sure . . . in the first place.": McClung, "The
        Social Responsibilities of Women," in "McClung
        Papers," in Savage, *Our Nell*, 81. (paraphrase)

194   "Mrs. McClung, don't you wish . . . wish that too?": Jane
        Brown John, daughter of Florence McClung, in tele-
        phone conversation 1998.

CHAPTER FOURTEEN

202   "help . . . not in vain.": Oke, "McCreary Man Recalls
        Kindness of Nellie McClung," *Western Producer* in Savage,
        Our Nell, 51.

202   "carload, stranded . . . Lake Winnipeg . . .": Based on a
        speech press release in "McClung Papers," in Savage,
        Our Nell, 66,67.

205, 206 "Sir Rodmond . . . to your credit.": McClung, 107.

206   "I know what . . . to see you.": McClung, 107.

206   "What in the world . . . meet a woman.": McClung, 107.

CHAPTER FIFTEEN

217   "Women do not have the executive . . . far too excitable.": Based on Nellie L. McClung notebook entry, in "McClung Papers," in Savage, *Our Nell*, 53.

218   "red-cheeked baby . . . radiant vitality . . .": McClung, 81.

218   "Another red-cheeked . . . well-tanned face.": McClung, 81.

218, 219   "You might as well . . . Meet the troops . . . ten months old.": McClung, 81.

219   "Four beautiful children . . . That's what you think.": McClung, 81.

220   "I was only sixteen . . . on you, Wes.": McClung, 209.

220, 221   "I heard about a skit . . . any too well.": Based on McClung, 113.

221   "delegation to . . . The delegation will . . . entirely of women.": McClung, 113.

CHAPTER SIXTEEN

222   "What a fine . . . These women were brought . . . those traditions are.": Based on *Manitoba Free Press*, 1, 28 January, 1914, in Savage, *Our Nell*, 86.

223   "I listened carefully . . . Where . . . given here . . .": Premier Roblin, in *Manitoba Free Press*, 1.

223   "I challenge anyone . . . Cheers from Mrs. Nash . . . *but* I can see reasons . . . our homes better?": Premier Roblin, in *Manitoba Free Press*, 1.

224   "The facts are against . . . to present them . . .": Premier Roblin, in *Manitoba Free Press*, 1. (quotation and paraphrase)

224   "if it is good enough . . . for anybody.": McClung, 117.

225   "brows beetling . . .": McClung, 117.

225   "women, queens of the home . . . superior to men.": McClung, 115,116. (quotation and paraphrase)

229   "Nellie McClung's Neglected (Children).": McClung, 126.

CHAPTER SEVENTEEN

233   "Roblin, Roblin . . . taste for beer.": McClung Campaign song, in "McClung Papers," in Savage, *Our Nell*, 96, ftn 15.

233   "the Old Maids' Convention?": McClung, *Purple Springs*
       (1921), 226.

234   "short-haired women and long-haired men.": McClung,
       114.

234   "asked to sign . . . to the government.": *The Winnipeg
       Tribune*, 29 January, 1914, in Savage, *Our Nell*, 88.

234   "Don't spare him . . . serious one!": McClung, *Purple
       Springs* (1921), 267.

234   "Ladies and gentlemen . . . Gales of laughter . . . And
       just to make sure . . . local colour.": Nellie L. McClung,
       in *The Winnipeg Tribune*, in Savage, *Our Nell*, 88.

235   "curtain rose . . . first session.": *The Winnipeg Tribune*, in
       Savage, 88.

235   "wearing a purple . . . white plume.": McClung, *Purple
       Springs* (1921), 267. (paraphrase)

235   "It was a protest . . . men's delicate hands.": *The
       Winnipeg Tribune*, in Savage, *Our Nell*, 88,89.

235   "father equal . . . with the mother.": McClung, *Purple
       Springs* (1921), 268.

236   "stand in well with the men!": McClung, *Purple Springs*
       (1921), 268.

236   "devote his life . . . this has been done—": McClung,
       Purple Springs (1921), 268,269.

236, 237 "I myself am keen . . . Well, then, are those . . . these
       gifts of love?": McClung, *Purple Springs* (1921), 269.
       (quotation and paraphrase)

237   "The Opposition is . . . positively indecent!": McClung,
       Purple Springs (1921), 269.

237   "leading a deputation . . . 'votes for men.'": *The
       Winnipeg Tribune*, in Savage, *Our Nell*, 89.

237   "A delegation of men . . . long-standing joke.":
       McClung, *Purple Springs* (1921), 269.

237   "The House . . . at the front.": McClung, *Purple Springs*
       (1921), 270.

237   "raised their opera glasses.": Based on McClung, *Purple
       Springs* (1921), 270.

238   "Come anytime . . . were the last time!": Based on
       McClung, *Purple Springs* (1921), 271.

238   "her hands in front . . . thumbs straight up." Based on

McClung, *Purple Springs* (1921), 271.

238   "We have the brains . . . us vote?": *The Winnipeg Free Press*, 29 January, 1914, in McClung, 121.

238, 239   "You, Mr. Babcock . . . church membership.": *The Winnipeg Free Press*, in McClung, 121.

239   "a cordial paternalism.": McClung, *Purple Springs* (1921), 271.

239   "Politics unsettles men . . . divorce!": *The Winnipeg Tribune*, 29 January, 1914, in Savage, *Our Nell*, 89.

239, 240   "Man has a higher . . . Nellie's voice shook . . . like a trumpet.": McClung, *Purple Springs* (1921), 274.

240   "Do you never read . . . cursed by manhood suffrage?": McClung, *Purple Springs* (1921), 274.

240, 241   "when they once get . . . The audience gasped . . . from the tombstones.": McClung, *Purple Springs* (1921), 275.

241   "Do you ask me to disturb . . . is political economy.": McClung, *Purple Springs* (1921), 275.

241–243   "The premier's voice darkened . . . Walking up and down . . . But I must not . . . The government supporters . . . I am building . . . Florence and Ruth . . . But, gentlemen, in spite . . . We are not worrying . . . never to defeat!": McClung, *Purple Springs* (1921), 276,277. (quotation and paraphrase).

243   "It was rumoured . . . votes for women.": *The Winnipeg Tribune*, 29 January, 1914, in Savage, *Our Nell*, 90.

CHAPTER EIGHTEEN

244   "great woman orator, the Canadian Joan of Arc.": *The Winnipeg Tribune*, 11 July, 1914, in Savage, *Our Nell*, 103.

246   "Well, if we don't . . . change the premier!": McClung, *Purple Springs* (1921), 215.

248   "There should be . . . on my feet.": McClung, 140.

249   "she went out . . . That must have . . . It did! She was . . . rights and privileges.": McClung, 186. (quotation and paraphrase)

249   "Nellie nodded . . . I will be." Jane Brown John, telephone conversation, 1998.

EPILOGUE

253   "was a feminist ahead . . . were not 'persons.'": J.L.
        Granatstein, "Nellie McClung: The 100 Most Important
        Canadians in History," *Maclean's*, 1 July, 1998.

254   "Nellie McClung, prairie reformer . . . let them howl.":
        Toronto Star, in McClung, *Clearing in the West*, back cover.